PILATES BABEL

A CITY ABOVE THE PLAINS

LEWIS DOWELL JR.

iUniverse, Inc.
Bloomington

Pilates Babel
A City Above The Plains

iUniverse books may be ordered through booksellers or by contacting:

iUniverse
1663 Liberty Drive
Bloomington, IN 47403
www.iuniverse.com
1-800-Authors (1-800-288-4677)

Because of the dynamic nature of the Internet, any web addresses or links contained in this book may have changed since publication and may no longer be valid. The views expressed in this work are solely those of the author and do not necessarily reflect the views of the publisher, and the publisher hereby disclaims any responsibility for them.

Any people depicted in stock imagery provided by Thinkstock are models, and such images are being used for illustrative purposes only.
Certain stock imagery © Thinkstock.

ISBN: 978-1-4759-5993-2 (sc)
ISBN: 978-1-4759-5994-9 (ebk)

Printed in the United States of America

iUniverse rev. date: 11/20/2012

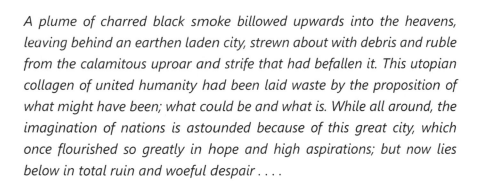

A plume of charred black smoke billowed upwards into the heavens, leaving behind an earthen laden city, strewn about with debris and ruble from the calamitous uproar and strife that had befallen it. This utopian collagen of united humanity had been laid waste by the proposition of what might have been; what could be and what is. While all around, the imagination of nations is astounded because of this great city, which once flourished so greatly in hope and high aspirations; but now lies below in total ruin and woeful despair . . . .

Pilates disturbingly awoke from a haunting dream drenched with an overabundance of perspiration and anxiety; he was perplexed by an edgy annoyance that was brought on by an absence of memory of the substance and meaning of the dream, which his abrupt awakening had not revealed.

"How much will that cost," the lady asked? "That will be one hundred and seventy five dollars," Pilates quoted to the woman. "That includes labor, parts and diagnostics. My rates are competitive compared to all of the other technicians that you might find because I am mostly a one man operation, so my overhead is low and the value of my work is very high." The woman smiled, crossed her arms over her chest and nodded her head in support of his price. "I replaced your hard drive; cleaned your circuit board for dust and debris and ran an antiviral diagnostic program on your system. The next time you install an antivirus program, be sure you get one on the higher end of the spectrum. They may cost a little more but they're usually worth it in the long run." The lady smiled sheepishly, saying she usually listens to her daughter about such things. She says she knows how to type and check her e-mail but when all those other images and messages appear with all that additional information crowding her screen; she goes phooey with a big sigh. Pilates laughs with her for a while. "They're just about making these things so that they can repair themselves. Believe it or not; they're almost about to put me out of business too. I can't complain though. I use 'em myself so if they are easier to use then that's better for me too."

After giving the woman a receipt, shaking her hand and saying goodbye, Pilates goes on his way feeling satisfied at another job well done. Now it's back to the office to regroup for the remainder of the day. He eyes his watch. It reads (2:00 pm). Maybe he has time for another 5 clients. It all depends on their systems and the problems they are having with them. While driving away from the house he'd just left in his service truck, Pilates mind wanders as it frequently does, to a recurring problem he has been turning over and over in his head trying to solve. The city had expanded so much, in such a brief period of time, with the rising population growth and the ever increasing influx of new cultures and groups of people of different backgrounds and walks of life; until it had proven to be a boon and a bane for his business. The language barrier had become his biggest challenge. Sure he took a foreign language in school just like everybody else; but just like everybody else, he was more focused on the grade rather than the understanding that maybe, just maybe, he would actually have to communicate with other people who spoke different languages than he did, in a real world scenario. So he muddles his way through some jobs the best he can. Just like the other day, there was this Russian lady, very bright and very interesting, who was also bilingual. The only problem was, when she reverted back to her native tongue; Pilates shook his head in disbelief at her assumption; she would converse with him in English for a moment or so before interchanging her speech back to Russian. She must have presumed that he could surely do the same in her language.

"Компьютер зависает все время, когда я в ней нуждается больше всего. Я пробовал все, что я знаю. Тем не менее, она просто постоянно идет на мгновение, когда мне нужно проделанной работе. Можно ли это исправить?" Pilates assumed she was referring to her computer because, after all, repairing her computer was the reason he was there; but he must have had one helluva quizzical look on his face while she was addressing him. The lady seemed to instantly recognize her mistake and reverted back to English in a blink of an eye so as to spare Pilates any undue embarrassment. She rephrased her question. "The computer freezes up all the time when I need it most. I've tried all that I know. Yet it just continually goes on the blink when I need work done. Can you fix it?"

"Yes ma'am," Pilates said dejectedly. He wasn't irritated at the lady of course. He was more annoyed with himself. His job was to repair peoples' computers. In order to do that, he should have had on his resume' an understanding of a couple of languages besides his own in order to be more competitive with the larger companies. He had his own business that included one other employee who did the clerical work while he did the field work. But, after pondering those thoughts for a while, he refocused on the task at hand and pushed those nagging worries to the back of his mind as other things in his life took center stage.

"John, before I come in, do you have at least 5 clients?"

"Yes I do Pi," John replied.

"Any of them over an hour?"

"You have one that may take that long. Looks like this gentleman is having trouble with his modem. Maybe it's a fried circuit board or some other wiring issue. You may want to schedule that one first."

"OK, give me that one priority A and place the rest in the order in which they were called."

"His name is Jose Costanzo. He lives at 1425 Demarco Lane off of Twin Oaks Rd- block #2010. I'm patching it through to your GPS now."

"Got it. Thanks John. Talk to you later."

'Ding dong. Ding dong'. "I hope Mr. Costanzo is home. It's just been twenty minutes since he called."

"Hola, ¿puedo ayudarte?"

"Hola, I'm looking for Mr. Costanzo."

"Yo soy su hermano José. Fue a la farmacia por un momento. Él debería estar de vuelta pronto. Hablo Inglés muy poco, pero mi hermano es muy bueno con Inglés. Él es el único que debe hablado antes."

"No hablan español."

"José estará de regreso en un momento."

"Maybe, there is another Costanzo living here. If he's out right now, I can come back. Someone called my office in need of a system repair for their computer."

"Ordenador. Computer. Sí. Sí. Entrar."

Pilates groans a little in his spirit. He hopes the other guy return quickly from whatever he is doing. He enters the apartment due to the gentleman beckoning motion for him to come in. He points to the computer. Mr. Costanzo shakes his head no and points to another room. Pilates anxiously follows, not knowing what to expect because of the miscommunication between the two of them. Yet, he wasn't unduly concerned about his own safety. He was more concerned about embarrassing himself. This guy might be talking about something else. Mr. Costanzo points to another computer and says, "Broken, broken". Pilates immediately understood the entire situation and opened his repair kit and started repairs. He only wished the other guy would return soon to ok the repairs before he got too far along in the process.

About thirty five minutes into the repair, Jose Costanzo appears in the living room, cheerfully greeting Pilates. "I'm sorry I'm late. I didn't think you would get here so fast."

"That's alright," Pilates replied, "I was out in the field so it didn't take me but a few minutes to reach your apartment. I really couldn't get too far along with your computer because you have to approve the work. This gentleman doesn't seem to speak English very well so I just peeked inside the modem for a preliminary look."

"Yes, said Jose. That's my brother Miguel. He's learning English now. He just needs more time. I was born here so I speak both English and Spanish."

"That's what I figured," Pilates explained. "I knew you must have been the one to place the order. Anyway I'll pull out your circuit board and test your hard drive. Maybe I'll find something in your wiring. It'll take a few moments for me to know exactly what's going on in there. OK?"

"Ok," Jose said.

After the repairs and finishing up his schedule, Pilates returns to the office to complete the final hour of his day.

"I'll tell you one thing John. I'm getting a little frustrated out there. I may have to hire an interpreter.

I know I can find Spanish interpreters and maybe Italian ones but I don't know about finding interpreters for some of those other languages I'm coming across out there. Most of the customers know some English. It's just me. I'll be the first to admit to my illiteracy in those other languages."

"Don't worry about it boss. The immigrant population is getting very literate in English."

"Yeah, I know but I just don't want to be left behind in all of this. Good night. See you tomorrow John."

"Good night boss."

Pilates heads home. This isn't the first time he has gone home with this particular topic in mind. He usually listens to John and shake it all off. But today, there seems to be a smidgen of urgency prodding him to resolve some of the unnecessary confusion that arises when he's out in the field. His small business is doing fairly well for the moment; but what if he hired more personnel? It would add to his total overhead of course and it would mean that he would have to adjust his prices. He would then have to hire other technicians. In other words, this notion seems to be leaning towards expanding his company, restructuring if you will. Ordinarily that wouldn't be such a bad prospect, expanding the company, but with the economy in free fall, the recession out of the window; Pilates knew this wasn't the time to expand his company. So, he needed to get off of that idea and try to do the best he could with the personnel he had. After all, who else could say they started their own business when they were just twenty years old and kept that company vibrant and flourishing for four years. He knew he didn't like to pat himself on the back very often but every once in a while he needed to hear the facts.

After Pilates got home, he tapped the button on his answering machines to listen to the messages forwarded to him from the day's queue. One after the other, the litany of messages filled in the spaces of missed calls. The next to last message caught his attention though: 'Hello Pi, I know you're at work. I just wanted to let you know I'm back in town. I would have called you later but I have some errands to do this evening. Hit me back on my cell later, when you've got a little rest. Talk to you later. Love ya. Bye.'

That was Misha on his answering machine sounding out laughter, joy and bliss; all wrapped up into one in each of her words. Pilates pondered how one can hear laughter in words. He reasoned to himself that it was beyond his comprehension or understanding. It was as if a smiley face came through his answering machine whenever she called. The biggest mystery of all was that each time she called; it seemed the exact same way. Without trying to, she made his frowns from the hectic demands of the day vanish. Pilates wondered if she even knew she had that ability with people. Everyone else who knew her said something almost to the same effect but they didn't quite put it into words the way Pilates thought best expressed how he felt about her. Their relationship was somewhat dubious for sure. She was a very good friend from their very first meeting but then she was a very good friend to a lot of other people as well. Pilates liked to socialize but he kept his friends to a small few. He felt it better to have a few friends you could totally trust and rely on when they were needed than many friends that are just there for you sometimes. He guessed that was how the world looked at it too. But take Misha; he was really romantically inclined towards her and he really wanted to be more than just her friend. She had many would be suitors and she seemed to always know how to keep them happy, but in the final analysis; they all had to eventually say, 'we're just good friends'. Pilates didn't know how she felt about being twelve years older than he was. He never felt comfortable or had the nerve to ask her about it. So he left it at that and joined the throng of all the others in saying, 'she's my best friend'. After all, he would rather share her company as a best friend than to not have her company at all. So he felt fully satisfied with the situation just the way it was . . .

Pilates' city was a sprawling urban community off the east coast of the United States with a population of around two hundred and fifty thousand people. It was located just on the outer rim of North Carolina. Hyperion's elevation was similar to the other cities in the surrounding area and was nestled between Durham, Fayetteville, Wilmington and Greenville. It was directly centered in the midst of these cities. It was long storied that it had an ideal climate most of the seasons in comparison to the droughts and floods and hurricanes that afflicted this area at certain times of the year. You might still find bits and traces of the locale and its culture and customs if you know where and how to look for it. Its name has not been recalled or spoken by residents of the adjoining communities for many years in recent memory. Maybe its name has been forgotten by design or by necessity. Either way Pilates has just begun to set into motion the huge cogs that turn the *wheels* of what must be.

"Hello Misha it's Pi. I just got around to calling you. I hope it's not too late. I tried your cell but got your voicemail. If you heard that message then you know I've been trying to get ahold of you. I'm glad you're back. I really missed you even though you weren't gone for very long. I hate to say that I might not get a chance to see you this time. I have to go to a seminar tomorrow. It's going to last for a week so I don't know your schedule; call me back and let me know how long you'll be in town. This seminar was scheduled well in advance so I can't cancel. Either way, I'll see you when I get back or I'll talk to you when you get back home. Love you. Hope to hear from you soon."

The seminar was for small, large and intermediate business owners specializing in high tech sales and repairs. Ever since he started his business, Pilates attended every seminar that was held. He was really looking forward to this year's events because he had finally gotten to the point where he realized that he had to ask some questions about certain issues that he needed answers to. Maybe some of the other attendees might have an answer to his problem. Anyway, there wasn't any harm in trying to get it solved.

The seminar began as usual with the representative updating the delegates on the latest technological news and gadgetry developments. Midway through his presentation, the rep stopped and asked if there were any questions. Pilates raised his hand and was acknowledged to proceed with his question. He asked the question about the increasing difficulty of social interaction with people on a larger scale due to the language barrier that was not only isolated to his city but that affected the nation as well as the world. The presenter nodded in agreement and went on to list all of the possible solutions to the problem. Pilates nodded as the presenter listed the choices that he could select from and their solutions. He had thought of all of the choices that were now being enumerated by the speaker. He waited for more. The representative said, "last but not least, you can always purchase the universal translator. It's the latest in technological innovation. When someone speaks to you, it interprets the conversation and translates it for you in a matter of minutes. It also translates your response to the conversation back to the person to whom you respond. Now how about that for innovation and convenience?" The crowd applauded the representative's solutions.

"I've heard something vaguely similar to it, maybe, when the item first came out; but recently I haven't heard any more about it. How much do they cost? I only need about two."

"They were a little more expensive when they first came out but the cost has gone down dramatically since then. I don't have an exact figure for what they're selling for now. Anyone?"

"I paid 900 dollars for mine," said one of the members in the audience.

"Six hundred dollars for mine," said another member.

"Well, there you have it," said the presenter. Now you can get with some of those members after the meeting and decide which one of those items is best for you."

"Thank you," Pilates said with a satisfied tone. That seemed to be the answer to his problem. He'll order two of them when he gets back; one for himself and another one for John.

The meeting adjourns and Pilates is eager to get back and begin a shopping search for the device. He should have thought of that solution before. It was such a simple and logical conclusion that Pilates thought he could have kicked himself for not realizing it before. He was going to order the translators first chance he got tomorrow morning. When he got back home; there was a message waiting for him on his answering machine from John, his employee and close friend, telling him he had a large priority A appointment schedule for a client first thing on Monday morning. He was instructed to go straight to the address for the maintenance and upkeep of a server module. He was told it was a very older model. Pilates scratched his head in wonderment. How old can it be? Johns' voice quickly told him over the machine. "Pi, I don't know what to make of this. A Mr. Archer called for service. After he explained to me the type of machine he had and the date and model,

I told him we don't service anything like that. I told him he needed to go to one of the larger companies and maybe he might have better luck with them. He said and I quote, 'My machine is very special.' He said it has seen military applications. He said it was constructed in the late '60's. I asked him how large it was and he told me quite frankly; it's the size of two large refrigerators. What would someone want with something like that is beyond me boss. However, he started talking about incentives, bonuses and perks! I told him I would have to talk to you about it. He wants you over there first thing Monday morning between six and nine o'clock. Call me back if you have any questions but basically, that's about all I got: Robert Archer. His address and phone number is on your scheduler. Hope you had a good seminar. Seems our business is more popular than ever. You've got a ton of clients waiting for you after you conclude with Mr. Archer."

Pilates was bewildered beyond belief. He was good with computers but this seemed to be a little out of his realm of expertise. After all he was just twenty four years old. That computer sounded like a relic from the cold war era. Why the gentleman wouldn't just go and purchase another computer was a mystery to him. Then Pilates reasoned with himself that Mr. Archer must be one of those trader buffs who keep old artifacts just for the fun of it. Pilates looked in his storage room and smiled at the neatly stacked computers; some of them even reaching upwards to twenty years old. But a refrigerated size computer; that seemed a bit of a stretch for an aficionado, even to Pilates.

Pilates spent the majority of Sunday evening browsing the web for any mention of the older type of computer he was supposed to repair, to see if he could find out a little more information on its basic structure that would help him determine the basic root of the problem. He hoped he could help the gentleman but he felt his knowledge of the machine would be surely even less than that of Mr. Archer. However, it was best for him to be there in person in order to arrive at that conclusion. Maybe there was something in all of this for him to learn about the machine as well. An interesting prospect without the need for compensation for his time spent exploring the machine.

Early Sunday morning Pilates arose and after showering; he got himself a cup of coffee and grabbed his repair kit and was on his way. When he reached the home of Robert Archer, he looked at his watch; it was precisely 5:45. He had fifteen minutes to spare so he grabbed a few notes about the older computers and scanned the information as quickly as he could. It wasn't that he felt ill prepared for the work; he felt any additional info would surely help him in the long run in diagnosing the problem.

At exactly 6:00 am, he ranged the doorbell. The door opened immediately but slowly. "Come in Mr. Daniels," Pilates heard the gruff voice say. "I've been expecting you. I have a Bowman series 9000 computer. It was built sometime around 1950-1960. I've been in possession of it for quite some time now. I bought it in vintage condition. Obviously, I know you can immediately appreciate and perceive my predicament, which is; how can I secure parts for my computer when the parts are now obsolete and are therefore no longer being mass produced for consumer use. So now that we've gotten that out of the way; what do you think of my Bow?"

Pilates gathered his thoughts. As soon as he entered the door he could see the gargantuan device. The monstrosity of the shape alarmed him at first sight in that it took up almost a whole wall space. Who needed something so large in this day and age, when they could very easily find a device that was ten thousand times smaller than his apparatus; a size more comparable to a composition notebook, that could do whatever this machine did and consume less power with less heat? Pilates grew angry at first, unable to speak, fearing he would say what he was actually thinking. "So you don't like my machine, huh," asked Archer?

"I've never seen anything like it," replied Pilates. "I've seen some older models before but they didn't quite come close to the size and shape of your machine. Is this a hobby of yours or do you belong to some kind of antique club?"

"No on both accounts. This is my everything."

"What?"

"Before we get into philosophy, religion or socialism, I would like for you *to peruse its features; decipher its codes and repair its shortcomings.*"

Pilates didn't like how Archer talked about the machine. He felt a growing annoyance at Archer that was steadily rising up inside of him. It wasn't professional of him to feel that way but he just couldn't help it. Here he was willing and ready to fix the machine and yet, Mr. Archer made him feel as though the main reason he was there was to resurrect someone from the grave.

"Forgive my manners," Mr. Archer said softly. "I live by myself and sometimes think out loud what others normally would keep to themselves. I know you're here to repair my machine so I'll leave you to it. Be careful if you have to go inside of it for any reason; the innermost parts are in very pristine condition but are somewhat tricky and very sharp-razor sharp. So do be careful. But of course you are so used to working on very small parts that this should be a piece of cake 'eh?"

"Just give me an hour to run diagnostics on it. Normally I wouldn't take that long but we've already established that your machine is rare. So I'll let you know in an hour whether I can repair it or not."

"Oh you can. I'm confident of it."

Pilates shook off what he wanted to say to Archer. He just wanted him to leave so he could find out what was really wrong with this piece of junk. He dismantled the outer casings of the machine and peered inside. To his surprise and amazement, the skeptical disdain he felt towards the outer appearance of the computer melted away as he marveled at the inner beauty of the machines' innermost parts. Sure, it had outdated parts like cathode ray tubes, halogen glass encased tungsten filaments and a circuit board equipped with antiquated circuitry, but it was just as Mr. Archer had explained; all parts were in pristine condition as if the machine was totally brand new. The opaqueness of the glass was so clear that the inside devices appeared in 3-D to his eyes. The assorted spectral scale of the colors were so lurid and provocative that it reminded him of a time when he was a youngster on Christmas morning; a time when upon arising from sleep, he would gaze through faint slumber filled eyes and see the brilliant tint and colors that were emanating from the tree and its ornaments and feel the magic and wonderment of life. It was that breathtaking! He plugged the machine in and heard a sound coming from it which should have been impossible for the apparatus to make. He heard a purring sound like maybe twenty cats, sleeping and stretching and yawning and cuddling. What kind of machine was this? What function did it do? Why . . . ?

While Pilates was deep in thought observing and experiencing the new sensations he got from the vibes of a different type of machine, he forgot the admonition of Archer. He slowly withdrew his arm from the cabinet. He felt no pain but to his amazement; blood dripped profusely from his elbow down his forearm onto the floor. He quickly grabbed a few of the rags he kept in his repair kit and bound his wound tautly. He eyed the floor and the pool of blood that was lying there just slightly outside of the computer's cabinet. He was relieved that Archer had a hardwood floor in that particular room. If he had been in any of the other rooms that were carpeted, he would have created a big mess. It wasn't going to be too difficult to tidy up this accidental mess though. Pilates prided himself on his work and the mere fact that this should happen at all, distressed him a great deal. He would keep it to himself and not mention it to Archer. After all he was bonded and everything and it wasn't like it was Mr. Archers' fault. He agreed with himself that it was entirely his fault; that he should not have been so careless in the first place. He now had to really rush because he was so far behind schedule that his hour for diagnosing the problem was almost up. He pulled out his volt ammeter and placed jumper cables on signet point A and signet point B. He scratched his head slightly. The meter indicator barely moved a centimeter. He turned on the monitor which was located in the center of the huge cabinetry. A small white dot appeared on the screen in the center of the monitor. In less than a second, the dot sped across the screen from *east to west*, making a full return twice before an image appeared. It must be his screen saver, Pilates reasoned. It was a simple image of clouds in the sky; puffy white clouds on clouds. Pilates had already come to the conclusion that he wasn't going to charge anything for the visit-no-not even charge a fee for the consultation. He still felt a little nervous about injuring his arm but if he didn't mention it to Mr. Archer, then everything would be alright. The puddle of blood was now gone with no indication that there ever was an incident at all. So he waited, sitting on his little work stool patiently, for Mr. Archers' return.

Archer came downstairs after about one hour and twenty minutes smiling as if he knew the news would be good. Pilates explained the situation; he told him that he could find nothing wrong internally with the computer; and he concurred with Mr. Archer that he did indeed have a very special piece of machinery. He told him that there would not be a charge at all for his service because he didn't repair it. Mr. Archers' face looked very perplexed. "Oh, but you have repaired it," he said. "I can tell just by looking at it. He turned on his computer. With a lilted tone coming from it, the computer said, 'good morning Robert.'

"Good morning Bo," Archer replied.

Pilates was happy the computer worked to Mr. Archers' satisfaction but now he was more than ready to leave. He noticed Mr. Archer reaching for his wallet. "Oh, no-no," Pilates said while holding up his hands to show his insistence on not receiving compensation for the work done. Yet Archer pulled out three one hundred dollar bills and demanded Pilates take it. He didn't feel right about accepting money for a job that he did not do very well. However, he started to feel the heaviness of the rags on his arm due to the absorption of blood accumulating on them; so he took the money in order to make a speedy departure. He really needed to get to an emergency room.

After leaving Archers' residence, he radioed in that he had to go to the hospital. An alarmed John inquired for all the details but Pilates kept it simple and professional. He explained he didn't think it was very serious. In fact, he said he believed that he may not even have to get stitches; he was just concerned about tetanus getting into the wound. However, Pilates wasn't concerned about tetanus as much as he was about getting the wound to stop bleeding. He doubted one could get tetanus from a machine in such pristine condition. He only wanted to allay any fears and anxiety that John may have had, so he felt it best to keep it simple. "Call my other appointments and let them know there will be a delay John. I'll call you back if I have to reschedule." Again, he heard the edginess in Johns' voice over the radio when he responded. "Are you sure you are all right Pi?"

"Yes John. I just don't know what the doctors may say. You know-take the rest of the day off or something like that; otherwise I'm fine. If I wasn't, I'll be telling you right now to cancel all of my appointments for the day."

"OK," John crackled in. "Call me back as soon as you're done at the doctors' office."

"Will do John." Pilates sped up on his way to the emergency room, hoping he didn't get a ticket on the way. Although he was a young man, he knew the value of keeping his driving record clean for professional reasons. Luckily he made it to the hospital without running into the police. He hurried into the entrance to the emergency room holding his right arm which by now had completely soaked through the light weight jacket that he had put on to conceal the wound from Archer.

The on duty personnel attendant calmly asked him to fill out some forms and then bring the forms back to the desk when he was finished. Although Pilates wasn't in any pain, he explained the situation as calmly as he could. He told the lady that he would have to use his right hand which was injured. He said the bleeding was so great that the blood would actually ruin all of the forms, making them unreadable. She quickly agreed while motioning for a nurse nearby to temporarily bandage his arm. She said that she would fill out the forms for him while the nurse stopped the bleeding. Pilates nodded his head and began to answer her questions. He only hesitated for a moment when he was asked the manner in which he had injured himself. "I am a computer IT Tech support agent and repair man. I was working on a computer and injured my arm in the process."

"Are you sure that's what happened," the woman asked Pilates?

"Yes ma'am," he replied.

"The only reason I'm asking, is because; it would take a computer of enormous size to do that much damage to your arm. They just don't make anything like that anymore."

"You're right," Pilates said, agreeing. "But, it just so happened, that was the case with me. I was working on a rather large older model and I just didn't pay enough attention when I withdrew my arm from the cabinet."

"Well we'll get you fixed up in no time and have you on your way," she said with a smile. Pilates hoped for that to be true. After they called him back to the examining area, a doctor came in to look at his arm. After carefully removing the bandages and wiping the area clean with a disinfecting solution, the doctor remarked that the wound wasn't ugly; meaning that it wasn't jagged or uneven in appearance. But, he said, stitches were necessary because of the depth and length of the wound. He said the skin would never completely heal itself unless the sutures were in place to aid in the healing process. Pilates didn't mind about the stitches. He was more concerned about the possibility of not being able to perform the necessary movements needed in his line of work. The doctor explained to Pilates," I'm putting you down for two weeks from strenuous labor with that arm. The tricky part is getting that elbow to the point where you can bend it normally again. That's going to take about an extra month of rehab. No muscles were injured, which is a miracle, considering how deep that cut is. It's a wonder more tendons and ligaments weren't damaged in the accident. Pilates didn't hear very much of what the doctor was saying to him after the duration of time was mentioned that he was going to have to miss from work. It wasn't so much the missing hours of compensation; he could always hire a temp to fill in for him for a couple of months to balance his worksheet. The fact of the matter was; he loved his job; he loved repairing the machines for his clients. He would do it for free if it were at all possible in todays' world. But it wasn't possible so he had to charge a fee. After the doctor gave Pilates a couple of pain capsules to take and a prescription for more; he asked him if he had any questions. Pilates refused the pain pills. He asked the doctor if it was natural for him not to feel pain in his arm. The doctor assured him that the pain was forthcoming; that he should make sure he got the prescription filled after he left the emergency room. Pilates half-heartedly agreed. He hadn't felt any pain since the accident which he thought was strange. The doctor mentioned something or another about injured tendons causing nerves not to send signals to the brain right away but for Pilates; it was all so simple. The cut was so deep and so long; he should have felt a great deal of pain immediately after it happened but he didn't. He prepared to brace himself for it in the morning. The pain may be so excruciating by then that it may become unbearable. He quickly had the prescription filled and headed home.

Once Pilates reached home, he checked in with John. He told him exactly what to do for the next few days: reschedule his appointments: check his temp list for a replacement IT tech and to remember to keep him posted, since it was only his arm affected and nothing else. He wrapped the cellophane plastic that the nurse had given him around his arm and took a nice long shower. After showering, Pilates went to bed and slept . . .

ένας κόσμος, ένα μυαλό, μια φωνή! ένας κόσμος, ένα μυαλό, μια φωνή!

The next morning Pilates arose, refreshed from the long restful night, ruminating on the phrase: one world, one mind, one voice! It was like a tune replaying itself over and over in his head. He felt relaxed from the peaceful sleep but annoyed at his inability to get that phrase out of his mind. He went straight to the television set and turned it on while trying his best to distract himself from the constant repetition of the phrase. He got himself a slice of an apple, a piece of carrot and a bottle of spring water and plopped down in his lounging chair while still clad in his pajamas and robe. He strolled through the channels slowly with no particular stop in mind, browsing for effect. He stopped on a certain channel; thinking to himself that this program certainly seemed different. 'Inspector, usted ha sido llamado por un crimen ha sido cometido. Es una responsabilidad muy grave, pero sé que varios asesinatos han ocurrido en esta zona. Continuarán ocurrir a menos que determinar quién es el asesino y capturarlo.'

'How many more persons must die before you act Inspector?'

'No more shall die. One way or the other I shall have your killer tonight!'

This wasn't a soap opera but it did a good job of getting that pesky phrase out of his head. Pilates smiled at the realization that he couldn't remember what it was.

Knock. Knock. "Who is it?"

"It's John."

"Hey John. Come on in. What's up?"

"I'm just checking on you Pi. Everything is running smoothly at the office. I got it on auto pilot. Our man is in the field completing your schedule from yesterday and all the new requests are being routed to him via his service list. So, how's it going with you?"

"I feel fine John. You shouldn't have come all the way out here. I appreciate your checking on me but you shouldn't worry so much. Worry will turn your hair gray."

"Yeah, I know. Hey, what's that you're watching?"

"Just some who done it crime drama. It's actually pretty good. I just caught about forty five minutes of it though. They're trying to find this serial killer who lives in the area. Nobody knows who it is. So the pressure is on the inspector to find him before he makes another fatal strike. You know . . . "Suddenly Pilates stopped in mid-sentence and looked at Johns' face. His head was cocked to one side and he had a baffled look on his face.

"What's wrong John," Pilates asked?

"How do you know what that program is about?"

"What? What do you mean? I didn't bump my head John. Remember, it's my arm."

"No Pi, I mean that program is in Spanish. That's a Hispanic network you're watching. Spanish all day-twenty four-seven."

"What? Look John, I appreciate you trying to cheer me up and everything but I know today ain't no April fools day. So what gives with you?"

"Seriously Pi, check the channel out if you don't believe me. You know you haven't been watching that channel. "Slowly Pilates diverted his eyes to the screen and saw to his amazement what John saw. He *was* watching a Spanish program. "So what, they must have just started translating the show which is a good thing, right? Hey, that's good they're translating it. Like I said, it's a good show."

"It's not translated Pi."

"What?"

"They're still speaking Spanish."

"No they're not. They're speaking English!"

"OK, let's see. I came all the way over here to cause you mental anguish by continually telling you something trivial about a TV show." Pilates knew better. John had a sense of humor but this did seem a bit of a stretch for him to pull some gag like that. However, there must be some explanation as to why the TV kept switching back and forth. Who knows; maybe they were having technical difficulties; anyway, it wasn't that big of a deal, where they should go on and on about a show. Pilates grabbed Johns' shoulder and apologized. "You know you had me worried for a while John. I didn't know if you were joking or if you were serious. You know these things happen all the time though. Just the other day while I was looking at a football game, the announcer was yelling 'touchdown! touchdown!' and the team hadn't even snapped the ball yet. You know what though? It was a touchdown play when they did snap the ball. Weird. Really weird."

"Yeah, you're right Pi; strange things happen with electronic devices. Hey, you should know. You fix them. Well, just like I said, I just stop by to check on you. I guess I'll get back to the office now. Oh, by the way, I almost forgot; Misha left a couple of messages for you at the office. I don't know why she didn't call you at home. She's one lady that's hard to figure out. Anyway, I forwarded the messages to you so you can listen to them when you get a chance."

"Thanks John. I'll give you an extra weeks' vacation when I get back."

"Yeah you do that. See you later Pi."

"Later John."

It had been a hectic few days for Pilates. He wasn't mentally or physically tired. It was just that things seemed a bit out of kilter for him. He liked things nicely arranged; cupboard neatly in layers. Yet since the seminar, he just hadn't felt the usual symmetry in his life. It probably was all just in his imagination but he kept getting the same creepy vibe over and over again.

With a lot of free time on his hands, Pilates, who usually kept busy most of the time, felt a growing need to sketch images and draw diagrams. He was using his left hand to draw and sketch the diagrams; so the dimensions and proportions of his drawings were a little curious looking in their appearance but there they were, ostentatiously lying in front of him; beckoning him to decipher their esoteric meanings. It wasn't an obsession or anything like that but Pilates did notice an increase in the bulk of the drawings. So he finally put them aside without ever looking at them as a complete unit. His arm was now beginning to heal. It never did really hurt. He hadn't taken a pain pill since day one. He didn't know if that was a good or bad sign. All he knew was that he was getting better; and that meant he was getting closer to the day he would be able to return to work. Little did he realize that the world he knew would never ever be the same for him again.

About a couple of weeks after his accident, Pilates went back to the doctor to get the stitches removed. He knew a little about stitches by being around a few people who had gotten them. He knew enough to know that with the number of stitches he had gotten, he should have experienced periods when the itching should have become almost unbearable. Yet he had no such episodes. There was neither pain nor itching and he had freedom of movement with his elbow joint. It seemed as if he had never even had an accident in the first place. And now here he was, sitting in a doctors' office, waiting to have his sutures removed from a wound that bore no resemblance to a wound at all.

It was a bright sunny day outside, while inside Pilates patiently waited for Dr. Marigold. He distinctly remembered the doctor's name because it reminded him of a flower. The doctor came in the room in a professional manner and pulled out a syringe. He pressed down on the top of the needle until it sprayed out a few droplets of mists into the air, and before Pilates knew it; the doctor was syphoning his blood into a vial.

"I'm here to get these stitches taken out," Pilates balked.

"Oh, don't be alarmed," the doctored said in a calm voice. "We are just cross referencing the hematoma from your last sample with this one."

"Why?"

"Well, we were looking for any foreign bodies that could have entered your blood stream through the wounds' opening on the date of your accident. We came across a few anomalous enzymes or antibodies or mineralogical unknowns. We thought it best to recheck. The labs-well not only the labs-but the medical database cannot ascertain what exactly these anomalies are or what they do. In other words this is more of a scientific discovery rather than a medical mystery."

"Why?"

"Because, you have no reactions, negative or otherwise at the injection site. By the way, that's a good thing. The mystery lies in the fact that we have studied samples of your injured cells and found that some of your enzymes do not match any of the known catalogued variety of enzymes that make up the total list. Obviously, it's a question we all want answered but not at the expense of your health; so we took this time to get another sample to cross reference with our last sample. I should have told you but the procedure falls well within the guidelines so we feel we are proceeding on the correct path."

That's the last thing Pilates wanted to become—a guinea pig. Anomalies, enzymes, antibodies, foreign objects, mineralogical unknowns; it just seemed a bit much for Pilates. It was just a cut and they made it seemed as if he were a medical marvel or an enigma. He hoped all of that nonsense wouldn't interfere with his business. The doctor explained that they would get in touch with him the very second they got news as to what the unknown elements were. In the meantime, he was to stay hydrated and to watch his diet. Pilates was always conscientious about his health. He ate healthy; went to bed early and got up early. He exercised until he hated himself. So what was the big brouhaha about? He felt as if nothing was wrong with him.

Back at home after he had gotten the stitches removed, Pilates noticed something about himself that he had not notice before. He was actually conversing with himself in his mind in a strange sort of way. He couldn't pinpoint exactly when it started or exactly what it was he was saying. It was a faint conceptualized interaction that bordered on conversations. One moment he was thinking about his business and then the next he was contemplating something that was vague even alien to him. He couldn't fully grasp the concept of what he was actually thinking about-not yet. It all became clearer to him later on when he ventured out into his normal sub routines. He would go to the supermarket to pick up a few items, only to become enmeshed in conversations with complete strangers for hours. Unbeknownst to Pilates, some of the very same people who he interacted with and conversed with so easily were actually speaking different languages than he was and yet, they understood one another clearly. It went on for a while until one day; Pilates was holding a conversation with a patron in the mall when another guy came up talking to the guy with whom he was conversing. He seemed to be upset about some money he felt he was owed.

"Who are you, man?"

"I am Pilates. Why?"

"This is none of your concern. This piece of dirt owes me money. I come to collect!"

The other patron looked to Pilates, as if he also wanted him to leave. Pilates sensed it was none of his business and was preparing to leave when he said, "I know it is none of my business. I know that money is important. I know we all come from dirt. I know we all have debts and I know that we all shall reap what we sow."

Both men looked curiously at each other and then at Pilates. One was Italian and the other was Polish. While both men spoke English, they each heard Pilates speak in their native tongue. The Italian heard Italian and the Polish heard Polish. Pilates heard only himself speaking what he understood. He wondered why both men departed so suddenly; each going his separate way without any other words being spoken. They merely walked away as if nothing ever had happened in the first place. It was a curious sight to behold; a nerve wracking sight; but it was an event upon which Pilates would remember in the coming months when he began his quest to recreate a system of one world, one mind and one voice.

Pilates grew less interested in his day to day business operations and began to focus all of his attention towards other things; things that at first sight seemed slightly irrelevant to him or to anyone else at the time, but they *were* very relevant. He finally sat down one day and placed all of his drawings on the floor as a mural of one big unit. He arranged the pieces of paper together so that he could view the bigger picture-the entire panoramic view. He saw four large satellites orbiting the earth; each controlling a section of one fourth of all the land mass. He didn't know exactly what it meant. He began to realize he had been drawing a lot of pictures with his left hand, thinking that he was merely doodling the hours away meaninglessly. He now saw in his drawings, masses of people from all around the globe, walking in unison side by side. Where were they headed, he didn't know, but he knew that something profound had occurred in his world and yet; he felt as though he did not possess enough intelligence to understand it all.

"Hello Pi."

"Hello mother, it's so nice of you to call."

"I haven't heard from you nor seen you in a while. Your father and I were getting a little concerned about you."

"There's nothing to worry about mom. I've been busy. I had to take a few days off from work . . ."

"I knew it! I knew something was wrong. I was just telling your father that you normally call at least once a week. Your father said to give you a little space; otherwise I would have called a lot sooner."

"I know mom. Tell dad I appreciate it. I did need a little time to myself. I hurt my arm about three weeks ago. That's why I haven't been going in to work."

"Three weeks? It's been more like six weeks haven't it! We haven't heard from you in six weeks."

Pilates thought for a moment. Didn't he just talk to John the other day? Yeah but John didn't mention anything about how long he had been absent from work. He had been so preoccupied with this new project until it had become very easy for him to lose track of time.

"I'm sorry mom; I didn't know it's been that long."

"If you haven't been going to work, what have you been doing to keep yourself so busy that you forget what day of the week it is?"

"I haven't forgotten what day of the week it is mom. I just didn't know it has been six weeks since I've seen you and dad, that's all."

"I ran into Misha the other day."

Pilates really did feel out of the loop. He forgot to check the messages that John had forwarded to him weeks ago.

"What was she talking about?"

"She said the most curious thing. She said she thought that you were over working yourself. She said she left several messages at your work and home but she never received an answer from you. John Palley called saying something similar except he left off the work part. How can you be so busy doing nothing?"

"It's not like that mom."

"Don't you mom me. Tell me what's bothering you."

"I had to get these stitches . . ."

"Does it hurt?"

"No mom, listen, they already took the stitches out. The cut has already healed. I'll show it to you when I come over. It's barely visible. It looks like a crease; like I've been laying on it for a while, that's all. I've been thinking about selling my business. I've been thinking about going into a new field."

"Whatever you think is best dear. You always had a head for business."

"Thanks mom."

"What for?"

"For being mom."

Encouraging words felt great even if she didn't know the full details of his future endeavors. She had confidence in him and that meant a great deal to Pilates. Pilates knew he didn't have all of the details himself but he knew where he had to start. First he had to make sure that John would stay connected to the business in spite of who bought it. That little clause would be in his provisions in the contract. After all, who would know the intricate details better than John about the day to day workings of the company. He was a great employee. Pilates was thinking of making him a partner before these series of events happened to him. He still thought of listing John Palley as co-owner when the business was sold. In that way, if the new owners were adamant about not taking him onboard, then he would receive some of the profits from the sale; just a little something to tide him over until he could find some other source of income.

Pilates scoured the internet looking for grants to sponsor his research. It didn't matter if it was private or government; he needed an advisor to steer him in the right direction. He also needed a technical committee to work out the many details his proposed plan would curtail. He needed to hurry with the sale of his business so that he could use the money from the sale as capital to fund a lot of the expenses he was bound to incur; until he received a monetary grant-if he ever did receive a grant.

After sending out numerous applications, he was invited to submit a grant application to a science research program. The program was a multi-lingual study of a large segment of society interrelated with a coordinated study instituted by the Regional Slate Foundation of Languages. He had a long conversation with his employee after receiving the invitation. He explained to John all about selling the company and all the computers he had amassed over the years servicing them. He told John about the clause in the contract insuring that he was guaranteed a job with the new company owner. However, John said he wanted to accompany Pilates on his new venture. He told Pilates that he could still be of some use to him with his new research program. John was getting on in years and Pilates knew that John didn't want to start all over with a new company. One of the reasons Pilates didn't ask him to accompany him on the new venture in the first place was the belief that maybe John was sort of tired of having a younger boss. John was sixty years old. He was old enough to be Pilates' dad but it didn't seem that way. It seemed to Pilates that John was the same age as he was, twenty four years old. But lately he had begun to discern Johns' real age. He was delighted to keep John with him. He told him so. He said their relationship would no longer be boss-employee but rather, they would become business associates.

"So you better ante up your share of the capital John to get this new venture underway," Pilates told him.

"How can I Pi, with the salary you pay me," John quipped back.

Now they were officially in the market for a new venture.

After Pilates' application was accepted, he was invited to an interview with Regional Slate Institutional Language Corporation. They were the largest foreign language teaching company in the world. They were number one in the sales of computer software, cassette tape, cds and every other media imaginable. Pilates met with a representative of the company named Mr. Richard Thornton. Thornton quickly got down to business.

"I have reviewed your application for a grant from our company. I have to say I am very impressed with some of your attributes. Although I see you have no professional foreign language studies whatsoever except what you mentioned on your application; the two years preparatory courses in high school, which doesn't count here by the way; you have managed to place in the upper echelon of our candidate list. You have had your own computer repair company for four years. You had two years of technical studies at an IT school. Yet somehow, you seemed to have aced all of our preliminary exams in linguistics. These exams aren't officially the basis upon which we determine whether or not a candidate receives our grant. We use these tests more as guidelines to determine who might better succeed in the job of bringing a better method of learning a foreign language to the masses. Our final decision rests solely on how well you do with the oral exam."

Pilates was a little confused. He was being interviewed for a staffing position at the company whereas he had applied for a grant for research instead. He wanted to explore the possibilities on his own and not as a paid staffer.

"So Mr. Thornton, whatever happened to your research grant?"

"This is the final phase now; you are one of the final candidates. However, our candidates must pass an oral exam. After you pass the exam, we determine how much your grant will be and how long your stipend shall last."

"My working environment, where will it be? Will I have a choice of independent research?"

"Those questions will all be answered after your exam."

Pilates felt a little rushed. For some reason, Mr. Thornton was placing too much emphasis on their tests. Pilates had a different goal in mind besides translating languages and interpreting them. For this company to be the largest language learning corporation in the world; something just didn't seem to add up.

He felt a little uneasy but it didn't seem rational for this large company to be doing something that wasn't completely above board. He didn't really want to go through with the tests.

"I respectfully decline to take your test."

"The only reason one would decline one would imagine, is the fact that you must have cheated on the preliminary exam."

"Is everything here about tests?"

"Yes, we must know our applicants qualifications and abilities. Then we can assess which candidate has the greater degree of command of the structure of the foreign language to be introduced into the area of the populace to be learned."

"Qualifications to do what exactly?"

"Mr. Daniels, I regret to inform you that your refusal to take the test disqualifies you for the grant."

"So be it then!"

"Good day."

Pilates was confused. He wanted to apply for a grant to do research. But now his memory seemed to fail him as to the purpose of the research to be done. That guy Thornton was some kind of language expert. He was talking about learning and teaching foreign languages. He was talking about interpreting and translating languages. Pilates knew what Thornton was talking about but he didn't know what he was doing there in the first place. He had to reexamine the murky plan he had. It just didn't make sense what he was trying to do. Thornton mentioned he had passed a test. He couldn't recall ever taking a test for their company. He applied for several grants, yet he couldn't specifically recall sending one to their business. It was like some nightmare where he couldn't wake up. For a brief moment, he felt like he was oh so close to his goal; only to have it snatched away with talks of tests and learning and teaching structures. Anger arose inside Pilates for just a brief moment. He knew he would do better the next chance he got.

Several weeks later, Pilates received a buyers' offer for his shop. He didn't want to appear overly eager to sell; which he was, but at the same time he needed to get the money from the sell quickly before the small faint inspiring voice left his mind. The offer came in at two hundred and fifty thousand dollars. Pilates felt he could have done better but acquiesced on the final amount. Everything was going to go with the sell except for four computers. He gave John two and he kept two. Pilates sent one last proposal to the government for a grant. He knew it was a long shot with the economy being the way it was but it was definitely worth a try. He received a reply in a very short time asking for figures, charts, diagrams and predicted outcomes. Pilates had all the necessary figures in his head. After giving all the information to John, who was an excellent typist, the information was on its way in record time.

In two weeks Pilates received a large manila folder. Inside were congratulations and a grant approval for two years with a stipend check of twenty five thousand dollars. In the total amount, the value was one hundred and twenty five thousand dollars for two years research. Pilates was now on his way to realizing the dream of one world, one mind, and one voice. Pilates placed three hundred and seventy five thousand dollars in his bank account with a sub listing of Daniels and Palley accounts. Now John was legally an equal partner in this research. Pilates knew he had to save the most difficult part of his plan for last so he started swiftly on the first and easier portion. He contacted NASA.

'Dear sir:

I am a private citizen requesting information on the protocols one must address in order to make use of your satellites. I am not talking corporation big but something as miniscule as a signal; a signal that will have matching corresponding points on earth at its axis in latitude and longitude. The signals must have a consensus of different governments at different strategic points around the globe as this exercise shall be one of coordination and progression. The signal must be the exact intensity because the entire population of the earth shall be receptive to its output. Please let me how much this will cost for the duration of two calendar years.

Sincerely,
Pilates Daniels'

Pilates knew NASA had a way of working with the science community around the world when it came to scientific projects. If Moscow agreed and India agreed, then Pilates could commence with the preparation of the other two satellites; one over North America and the other over Europe. Pilates' project began to pique the interest of certain inquisitive groups. One such group was the company Pilates had already had dealings with. Regional Slate Corporation was by now keenly interested in Pilates' project for some reason. They were very low key in their surveillance but they were prepared to step it up if Pilates plan grew more ambitious.

John began to sense the hugeness of Pilates' aspirations and wondered if Pilates knew exactly the consequence or repercussions of such a lofty task.

"Pi, what do you hope to accomplish at the end of all of this research?"

"John, I thought you and I were on the same page all along. I apologize if I left out some detail. I told you as much as I know."

"Yeah but now, it's getting a little scary. I'm seeing a picture-an ecumenical picture where something is bending in the wrong direction, causing individualism to disappear. If that does happen, we will be in some kind of a mess. It's unprecedented. Mass hypnosis. Mass cooperation. Unilateralism. The worst part of it may be the governments of the world may actually allow all of this to happen."

"Are you with me John?"

"Always, but up to a certain point. I'm not going to allow you to destroy yourself. You should talk to some of the intellectuals, the theologians and philosophers before you do this."

Suddenly Pilates experienced a flash of deja vu. He was back in the home of Robert Archer. He remembered Archer mentioning religion, philosophy and socialism. It was such a fleeting moment for Pilates, he barely noticed the inhalation, exhalation moment. Just like that it was gone; he couldn't remember another thing along those lines.

"What's particularly bothering you John?"

"You haven't given or at least I haven't seen a conclusion to your proposal. I mean did you ever put it in the materials I sent off for you?"

"The reason I didn't put it in the proposal John is because there is a sensitive and complicated element to the entire final process. It's needed but I just haven't figured out the best approach. You know I will tell you when I decide which approach is best."

"Wouldn't you make a better decision if you had other peoples' input?"

"I see what you're saying John and I know exactly how you feel. The truth of the matter is ; the last component of my process includes my blood."

"Say what? What?"

"Don't freak out on me John. I'm not talking about ritualistic sacrifices or martyring myself."

"That's a relief. What exactly are you talking about Pi?"

"It's a long, long story."

"I think it's about time you told someone, don't you?"

"Alright. You remember Robert Archer?"

"Somewhat vaguely."

"The place where I hurt my arm."

"OK. Oh yeah I remember him."

"Well something happened to me that day. The reason I'm not telling you more is because I don't know anything else either. I'm still waiting on information from the medical and the scientific community. They're onto something but they're not letting on to what they know. I feel a certain urgency to get this thing up and running. I may not have a lot of time left. Who knows. They didn't tell me that but they made me feel that when they did come for me; it's going to be all out. They're going to make me a guinea pig for their research. They might as well have come out and said, 'hey, we want your blood.'"

"You should have told me Pi."

"What good would that have done. Look at you. In the last six months your hair has gone from stark black to platinum grey."

John rubbed his fully platinum hair and sighed, knowing Pilates was telling the truth. But he couldn't' afford to let up.

"OK. If we're *gonna* do this, then we *gotta* do it right. First, no more secrets. Second, list all of your steps when you get a chance so if you have a memory lapse, they'll be in writing where we can see them and keep on working. Deal?"

"Deal."

Pilates became fastidious in his record keeping after his conversation with John. He began to think it was better also, to always document his facts and record subsequent steps taken. After all, who knew if the committee would come in one day and demand verification of his procedural hypotheses and their expected solutions.

While Pilates enmeshed himself in his work, Dr. Marigold had received startling news concerning the medical samples that he had collected from Pilates. The return information came back marked 'Top Secret'. He pressed for answers for the reason the 'Top Secret' status was merited. Was his patient in any peril? Was the classification due to a contagious disease? He was told that the case was no longer his. He was told to forward all the documents and charts about the patient to a certain panel. Dr. Marigold refused, citing patient/doctor confidentiality laws. They returned a more ominous sounding message stating that they were representing the highest level of governmental authority.

"Ron, I say we can't let them get away with this; some secretive panel, hiding in the shadows, threatening us with rank and file. He was my patient and he deserves to know what's going on. We're just as much in the dark as he is."

"What do you want me to do Tom? They presented the credentials. It went as high as the surgeon generals' office."

"I can see if it was only the surgeon general but they had a physicist name also joined to the bloc of other names. I have never seen anything like it. You know the procedures we have to take if there is a genuine threat to public safety. You're the administrator of this hospital! You make the call in conjunction with CDC instead of them making the call!"

"Why are you taking this so personal? This is very highly irregular for you."

"I am inquisitive. I want to know what it is that this patient has too. It's like in the olden days when a homesteader reached a certain spot of land. If he was there first, he could claim homesteaders' rights and the land was automatically his and his alone. This was my patient and whether by accident or by design, I should have the first-hand knowledge of what the great mystery is. It's not a disease. It's not anything we know about. Now they're saying they know. How can they know? Where did the knowledge come from; to suddenly say they know what it is now?"

"Don't beat yourself up over this Tom. There's probably a logical explanation. There have been times when I was dumbfounded myself about certain things, but you know what; I found that most of those times there was a simple explanation to everything. The fear of public panic or the recalling of massive quantities of products could lead to mass hysteria. We just don't know. I caution you to let this go. Give them what they want and let the problems go with it. You are no less of a doctor for following protocol."

"Alright Ron."

There was a huge buzz going on in the science community of a *special* particle being recently discovered. They called it a *boson*. It seemed that the sample that was sent away containing Pilates' blood was adding to the excitement and uproar. They wanted to put a lid on the situation quickly by isolating the individual who so uniquely delivered to them an elusive element for which they had been searching for nearly half a century, so that they could protect him from all harm. This particle that was located within his blood cells was very special indeed.

However, Pilates was two steps ahead of them without even being aware of their plans. By now the other sector of the government, the one that had issued the grant to Pilates, was completely giddy over the progress that was being made by his group.

Word spread far and wide until it reached the ears of the committee members of a branch that included service to humanity and awards. One such member was Jim Bainbridge. He headed the scientific panel for compiling names of potential Nobel Prize nominees. Once Pilates' name crossed his desk, it was Bainbridge' job to investigate the credibility of the program and to weigh its intrinsic value as opposed to certain other programs of scientific endeavors. He would then forward the name or names to a larger committee in Norway. There in Oslo, they would then put the candidates' achievements to the ultimate test to see who would become the winner of the Nobel Prize for science. Bainbridge followed Pilates' group for a week. Pilates was amazed at the questions he was asked. It seemed to Pilates as if he were talking to John all over again. Bainbridge asked him the same questions that John had asked him; what did he hope to achieve in his project and by what means would he achieve them. Without even realizing it, John had given Pilates a dress rehearsal for that particular moment.

Although Bainbridge gave Pilates a reason for following his work, not once did he ever mention that Pilates and his group were being considered for the Nobel Prize for science. He told them leaders in the science community were genuinely intrigued by their work, which was true. He also told them that those same leaders were interested to see the outcome of such a mammoth project, which was also true. After spending the entire first day with Jim Bainbridge, Pilates turned over all of the rest of the information sharing to John and his assistant Peggy. Even while he was very busy with the project, Pilates still multi-tasked every day with the querying thought, 'one world, one mind, one voice'.

Agents from the Regional Slate Institute were reporting back to Thornton that Pilates' enterprise had grown immensely. They said they were seeing more enthusiasm coming from the growing number of people who wanted to know more about what was going on inside of his complex. After hearing the report, Thornton called an emergency meeting of the senior members of his council. They numbered twelve altogether. Whatever went on in those proceedings among those twelve council members never left the room. They were bound by secrecy; sworn under oath to never reveal the secret upon which their whole institution was built. The rest of the Regional Slate Corporation had no clue to the rules and history that had been entrusted to these twelve members.

"Gentlemen, I called this meeting due to some alarming news that I have received most recently. There was a young man who applied to our company a while back. He said he wanted to receive a research grant. I have never seen such perfect scores on any of our exams before in my lifetime; so I proceeded to test him further, to verify that his scores were registered accurately. The young man grew angry for no apparent reason and refused our tests. I may have been a little hasty when I indirectly implied that he may have cheated on the exams."

The whole room made a 'whooo' sound. "Gentlemen, gentlemen please, that is beside the point. The point is, if he did not cheat; he must have in his possession the SLATE!

The members' demeanor changed in a blinking of an eye. They went berserk ripping and tearing at their clothes. Thornton did not try to calm them down as his face now took on a more ominous look of concern. "The tiny portion of the SLATE that we have, must pale in comparison to his portion of the SLATE; because he grew angry at the thought of translation! He grew mad at the mention of interpretation! He said amen to the possibility of misunderstanding!" The members were now completely out of their minds with uncontrollable rage. They wanted to kill Pilates. Thornton, perceiving their hearts, spoke to them as if it were by mental telepathy. 'We shall let the courts deal with him'.

The room calmed down.

Pilates sat in his room in deep concentration. They were nearing the final and most crucial juncture of their endeavors. If only he could synthesize that unknown ingredient in his blood which was the catalyst for the entire operation; it would make the final stage work. He didn't know what to look for or how to go about getting to that mysterious element. He concentrated and hoped. Suddenly he opened his eyes and beamed the biggest smile anyone could ever imagine. He had received his answer.

Now if only he could get his plan to work. He left their working environs and headed to the hospital; hoping and praying that he could convince Dr. Marigold to help him. After he got to the hospital he asked for a consultation with Dr. Marigold.

"Hello Dr. Marigold."

"Hello Pilates."

"I guess you're wondering why I am here."

"Actually I was hoping to see you again."

"You never got back in touch with me doctor like you said you were going to do."

"It's complicated. I had to transfer your case to a higher authority."

"Why?"

"I'm not allowed to discuss your case anymore, not even with you."

"Sounds like a conspiracy to me Doc."

"I agree. I'm going to tell you everything I know. Just promise, you didn't hear it from me."

"I promise."

"I think they're trying either to set you up to be a top secret guinea pig or they're going to slice and dissect you for study."

"Sounds very morbid to me doc. Can they do that without my consent?"

"Normally no, but when national security, call of duty and the public safety become sound boards, then you don't stand a chance."

"Well doc, they can do what they want to me after I get my project off the ground."

"What project?"

"That's the reason I'm here. I was hoping that maybe you'd give me a helping hand."

"How can I help?"

I need you to do the exact same procedure you did before, except this time; I want you to personally screen my samples for all of that stuff you were talking about before. When you find the unknown element that you are looking for; I want you to try and isolate it so that it stands alone from all the normal antigens. Can you do that doc?"

"Yes, but what in the world do you want that done for?"

"I'll purchase all the supplies that you need and pay you for your efforts."

"I don't think it's such a wise idea to pay me. I could get into a lot of trouble for that. Since you're not my patient anymore, I can do that for you on my downtime when I'm off the clock."

"Great. Let me know when it's convenient for you doc."

"I still have your number. I'll call you later today after I check my schedule. Alright?"

"Sounds good to me."

It was almost too good to be true. Pilates had solved the last piece, the most difficult piece of the puzzle. While he was concentrating, trying to come up with a solution for the final step, a picture of a marigold flower appeared in his mind and that was how he knew he had to go and see the doctor. Now, once the doctor isolates that element, he could then simulate it in some kind of way. Pilates stopped and thought for a moment. He remembered the doctor telling him that the enzyme was unknown. If it were unknown, then how could that unknown be duplicated? It made Pilates head hurt to think past that point. He resigned to himself to let the doctor help him and go from there. The doctor was very smart. He probably would have the answer after he saw first-hand what Pilates intended to do.

"Hey Misha, what in the world are you doing here?"

"You don't return my calls. You don't answer my texts. Your mother told me where I could find you. She said you were very serious about some project. I said, project. She made it sound like you're a mad scientist or something. IT'S ALIVE! IT'S ALIVE! Don't tell me you lost your sense of humor Pi. So what have you been up to?"

"Well, I have been very busy. But I'm not that busy that I can't say I am happy to see you again. You're like some globe trotter zipping in and out of town ever so often. What do you do now?"

"If I told you . . ."

"Yeah I know. You'd have to kill me."

"Correct. I don't want to kill you though. I want to love you. Kiss me."

Pilates awoke on his cot. He had fallen asleep for a few minutes-twenty minutes tops. It seemed as though he had slept a lot longer. He felt well rested. He couldn't remember what he had dreamed. It must have been something pleasant though because he was still feeling all warm inside. 'Knock. Knock.'

"Come on in."

"Are you sleeping Pi?"

"No, not now. I dozed off for a few minutes. What happened?"

"I hate to bring you bad news but this doesn't look too good."

"What's that?"

"It looks like a summons to appear in court. A deputy dropped it off a few minutes ago. I didn't read it. Open it up. Let's see what this is all about."

'Pilates Daniels:

You are hereby summoned to appear in district court nine on the twelfth of July, 2012 to answer to the charges brought henceforth against you by the Plaintiff: Regional Slate Language Institute Corporation.

You must answer to the charge of sabotage; divulging corporate industrial trade secrets and corporate theft.'
Docket#567845

Pilates stared at the summons, wondering it they had the right person or not. Then a slow sinking feeling yanked at his stomach as he realized that the charge was from the same company that he had an interview with. There must have been some mistake. He was barely in that building for two hours. How could they say he had done all of that in a brief two hours. He wished the doctor would hurry and give him a call. He had a bad feeling about that Regional Slate Company.

When the mail arrived, Pilates looked through the usual mail: bills, bills, charities and bills. Then across a long sleek envelope, Pilates noticed a golden trim. It was from Jim Bainbridge: Nobel Prize selection committee. He opened the letter not knowing what to expect . . .

'Congratulation recipient:

You are hereby notified that under close consideration with undue scrutiny, you are selected as the final candidate for this year Nobel Prize for science.'

Pilates stood looking at the letter in disbelief. He had gotten horrible news and the best news of his life in the span of one hour. He glanced at the remaining portion of the letter which gave him the time and place the award was to be presented. He saw the stipulations.

It told him he would receive travel allowance for a round trip to Oslo, Norway. Pilates was now more determined than ever to get his project off of the ground before either his court date arrived or before the date his award was to be presented.

When Dr. Marigold finally arranged to meet with Pilates, the time and locale was kept secret in order to avoid detection. He told Pilates that his phone may have been wiretapped from the very first day his file was listed as Top Secret. He also informed him that he may have been the subject of a surveillance operation ever since he was tagged with a classified file. Dr. Marigold explained to Pilates that he would use a code name when dealing with his case so that he would not raise the suspicions of the surveilling authorities. Pilates thanked the doctor again for helping him. The doctor confided to Pilates that his reward would be to see the resolution of the mystery surrounding his case. He promised he would get it done as quickly as he could.

Dr. Marigold kept up his end of the deal. After acquiring the correct sample from Pilates, he shipped them under very heavy security and with a large insurance guarantor to Geneva, Switzerland. They were shipped to the care of the addressee: Dr. Carusio Moitreti: Director/C.E.R.N./ European facility. The letter accompanying the samples, explained in greater details the points Dr. Marigold had already discussed with Dr. Moitreti in e-mails and by telephone conversations. He finished his letter by acknowledging that he knew that Dr. Moitreti was a very busy man. He thanked him for his time and intimated to him that he should keep all of their further correspondence strictly confidential.

Needless to say, when Dr. Moitreti received the shipment, he immediately initiated the necessary experiments in the hadron collider. It was on the very first attempt that he received an answer. It was to his great surprise, the *Higgs boson*. He knew where the samples that he was using in the experiment had come from. He also knew that it was impossible for the data, which the computers were compiling, to be correct. He ran the test at least ten times; and ten times, the data remained the same. He sent an encrypted e-mail to Dr. Marigold, asking for more information about the subject from whence the samples had come. Dr. Marigold returned an encrypted e-mail reiterating that the source that the sample came from was human hemoglobin.

The answer to the problem, as Dr. Moitreti deduced, was to excrete the bi-product from the hadron collider chamber into a plasma form. As long as the correct container was used to store the particle, the principle properties of the element would retain their energized fields until they were propagated into whatever medium they were to be engaged in. He instructed Dr. Marigold to preserve a large amount of the hemoglobin because he was excited beyond sanity to be able to engage in experimentation with that newly discovered element. Dr. Marigold assured Dr. Moitreti that he needn't worry; he informed him that when Pilates got his project up and running; there would be an ample supply to be shared by all.

Misha Barton turned on her large flat screen television to catch a few moments of the days' news. She was wearing her usual gray flannel warm up bottoms with a white shirt girded about her midriff into a small knot baring her belly button. She held a very large goblet with a very small amount of claret in the glass with her hands. Sliding onto her large comfortable sectional couch with her feet curled under her body; she twirled the small amount of liquid around and around in her glass as if by just sniffing its tart aroma gave her great pleasure. While flipping through the news channels, she stopped abruptly and returned to a channel that had called out a name-a very special name.

'Well Bill, this story should touch base with a lot of young entrepreneurs out there. A local resident here in Hyperion seems to have become almost an overnight success story. Pilates Daniels' name has been on a lot of peoples' mind as of late. He's scheduled to receive the Nobel Prize in science; and he is scheduled to bring about a creation that will probably put a lot of people out of work also.

But that's the downside to it. The upside of it is; his creation may change our whole economy, our social structure and maybe change our entire world. According to the Science Monitor, he proposes to give us the means whereby the entire world can communicate without translators or interpreters. Seems farfetched? Maybe not. Historians and Theologians have long held the belief that in mankind distant past there was one universal mode of communication . . .'

'That's right Erica, until Babel.'

'What?'

'Babel, Erica, Babel, you know the biblical story of The Tower of Babel.'

'I must not have read that story. And I do apologize to our viewers but Bill never mentioned it while we were preparing for this story.'

'Don't worry Erica; it's not a topic that's heavily discussed today. I was just wondering if Pilates Daniels ever heard of it. It seems he's trying to recreate something that God disallowed before.'

'That's very interesting Bill. So you're saying God doesn't want people to understand one another?'

'That's what happened before. Maybe our viewers can call in and give us their point of view.'

Misha sat upright wondering if she heard right. They called Pi's name. They called his city. She stared intently at the television screen for more information.

'We have our first caller: Reverend Jerry Dennard from Charlotte, NC. Go ahead Reverend, you're on the air.'

"First of all I don't think this is the proper forum for discussing these matters. It's interesting to note that you started off your program as if you were going to report the news of a local story in Hyperion. I noticed you added a bit of skepticism into it and then invited others to sprout opinions about God's word. You don't go to a car dealership and ask the salesman about giving you advice on repairing your house do you?"

'Bill, I think we have a live one here.'

'Sure looks that way Erica.'

'So Reverend, what do you say about it?'

"I say if God didn't want people to be able to understand one another then he wouldn't have given them the universal speech in the first place."

'What do you say to that Bill?'

'With all due respect sir, you're talking about before Babel. Once it was taken away, He didn't want you to have it. He . . .'

"Bill, you have a finality in your voice. You mean you can't understand that God can reserve a thing to Himself to be reinstated at another time when He knows one is ready to receive it?"

'He has a very good point there Bill.'

"Excuse me. I just called in to voice my opinion about the forum of the discussion and not to join in. I think these matters should be approached with dignity and within the confines of a proper environment and not for entertainment sake."

'Thank You sir. And we do appreciate your input. Next caller.'

Misha eyed her phone. She wanted to know more about Pi. The newscasters knew a great deal more about Pilates but it seemed they were more interested in talking about philosophy and religion than telling the rest of his story. Misha caressed the phone gingerly; intertwining the cord intermittently between her fingers. If she called, she wasn't going to tell them she knew Pilates. She wanted only to find out what it was all about. Nobel Prize. That was something!

"Hello."

'Hello'

"Yes. My name is Misha Barton."

'Hello Misha. Where are you from?'

"I'm from New York."

'What do you think about our topic today?'

"I think it's a fascinating story. How did Pilates Daniels accomplish all of that in the time frame which he did? Which university did he go to and what was his primary field of study?"

'Well Misha. That's the extraordinary thing about this story. According to our notes, he came out of nowhere virtually overnight. That's the first thing we checked on. His background shows no doctorate degree, no masters and no foreign exchange experiences. It's a mystery. But the people who know all about it are saying that he is very credible. They say that if he can do what he says he can; we may very well speak in that original tongue that they spoke in the time before Babel.'

'There you go with that Babel again Bill.'

Erica, it's right there in front of you. That's what he says in his proposal. That's why they're giving him the Nobel Prize.'

"Excuse me guys, you don't think it's odd that he can do that? I mean you don't just go from speaking one language in one day and then all of a sudden speak; how many languages is he able to speak now?"

'That's the strange part Misha. Although we didn't get this information first-hand, we heard from a reliable source that he already has the capacity to speak seventy two languages. He is striving to do away with all seventy two languages though. According to his proposal, there shall be only one voice.'

"What?"

'We took it to mean one speech, however, you're welcome to opine your thoughts on what you think he meant by it.'

"Thank you but I got what I was after."

'Erica, seems the Reverend has frightened all our viewers away.'

'So it would seem Bill.'

It was all too much for Misha to absorb at once. She knew Pilates. Although she found him to be witty, adorable and sweet, she just didn't picture him as a brainiac type or someone who could come up with such a mind boggling idea that it made the most creative minds of our time stop and take a look and say 'huh'. She couldn't fathom the depth of what the television commentators were saying so she decided to get the meaning of it all from the source, Pilates, himself. She left her television set on while she went into the bedroom to pack a few things for the trip to North Carolina. She wanted to find out what exactly had happened. She wanted to personally congratulate Pilates for his accomplishments but mostly she just wanted to see him again.

While she was packing, she heard something on her television set that didn't quite enter her ears in just the right way. She stopped packing her suitcase and listened. 'Well Bill, you know what they say, you can't have roses without the thorns. To comment on that story we were sharing with our viewers earlier, we just got word that Pilates Daniels is to be arraigned in a court proceeding. Although it appears to be a blue collar crime, we were informed that the charges are very serious. If convicted he could face up to twenty years in prison. That's a big turnaround from the story we reported earlier. This latest news could cause the prize committee to rethink their decision. It's too early to tell but we'll definitely keep an eye on this story and update you as we get more information. That'll be a shame Bill if they find him guilty.'

'Yes it would be Erica. I understood that this was going to be an historic event-a once in a millennium type event. If he *is* guilty, he surely had a lot of intelligent people fooled. And it's just like you said Erica, he could lose his prize award. So stay tune to this developing story.'

Misha dropped the articles of clothing that she was preparing to place in the suitcase on the bed. She only paused momentarily to catch her breath. She felt she needed to go to North Carolina now more than ever. She was on her way to see Pilates at first to congratulate him but now she would be going to offer him her support. She knew the type of person Pilates was. He would never in a thousand years do anything like what they were accusing him of doing. In fact she knew just the lawyer who Pilates should get. Her lawyer was one of the very best in the business. He went to great pains to defend, in his estimation, only those who he honestly believed to be innocent. He wouldn't take the case no matter how much money he stood to gain, if he felt that the client was actually guilty. So he mostly got his clients indirectly from the family and friends of the accused. The more time his clients faced, the harder he fought for their rights. She would e-mail

Pilates the referral name of her lawyer. She also offered to assist with any expenses if he needed any help. She knew Pilates would decline her offer for monetary assistance even if he needed it but she had to make the offer just for her own peace of mind. If he was desperately in need of help, he may just have to take her up on her suggested financial help. She sent the e-mail.

Pilates was a little concerned now that maybe the committee would rescind their offer to him for the Nobel Prize after they heard the news of his impending court appearance. He was counting on the monetary reward to offset some of the costs he had incurred with his project. That money would have also allowed him to move up the date and time for the project initialization. However, Pilates didn't have to wait in apprehension very long. The scientific community was so anxious to see the outcome of his experiment, that they wouldn't let some impending courtroom drama keep them from witnessing that outcome. Plus, there was the matter of the other bloc of committee members who were also keenly interested in Pilates from a medical/scientific standpoint. They were the same members who had surveilled Pilates after he had the incident where he injured his arm. So Pilates had quite a number of influential people who were behind him one hundred percent.

Yet, for all those people behind Pilates, supporting him in his endeavors, there were twice as many foes, lurking in the shadows that opposed him at every turn. He had only met a few of them and he didn't realize at the time that they would soon become his mortal enemies. Regional Slate Corporation followed the news closely about Pilates' meteoric rise to stardom and fame. They believed that he had acquired an artifact hundreds of centuries old similar to the one that they had. The meager remnant they had in their possession was carefully preserved and stored in a vault in the basement cellar of the Slate building. They were carefully chosen for the solitary task of overseer of the relic. The identity of their number one leader was always a mystery. Not one of the twelve members had ever seen him. However, their leader had some mysterious means by which to communicate with the director of the corporation.

Richard Thornton was the director of Regional Slate Corporation worldwide. Although he had never seen the CEO of the company, it appeared he knew the directives of the CEO down to the letter. The twelve council members were the only employees of the company who were permitted to see or touch the Slate. Out of the entire company worldwide, only they knew the existence of the Slate. Even Thornton did not know the origin or the history of the SLATE. It was a sliver piece of metal shaped in the form of a half triangle. It was the size of a small stapler with a thickness no larger than two centimeters. Its dull grayish matte hue made it appear as though it were an ordinary piece of stone. Judging by the way the members acted whenever they were in its presence though, one would have to conclude that it must have possessed a great power. It was almost as if the stone was worshiped or revered so much by the twelve members that if it ever were to be lost or stolen, the world would come to a very abrupt end for its members. So it was kept under constant guard twenty four hours a day, seven days a week, by electronic surveillance in addition to armed personal guards. With a time lock vault installed, the door opened only at pre-configured times of the day when two or more members could enter. Even Thornton could not gain access to the room alone. On this day, Thornton had a group of people in his office, rehearsing for their role in the upcoming legal attack on Pilates Daniels. They memorized their lines and listed dates and times for certain events and occurrences. Thornton judged their appearances and their believability. He graded them and coached them. This group was hired with the sole purpose of discrediting Pilates. After the trial, they were to each receive a ticket to their choice of destinations in the world, where they would be listed as salaried staffers to the company; but they would never have to report to work ever again a day in their life.

Pilates meanwhile had received his invitation with a note that he could bring three guests with him to the awards ceremonies. He already knew John was going and Peggy Lee, his assistant would accompany them; that made two. He could always ask his mother but then he thought, he didn't want to leave dad out either. It was a dilemma and he didn't want to waste the ticket but the main thing for Pilates was to prepare his acceptance speech and go get his award so that he could get back quickly to the business at hand. He didn't have time to worry about an extra ticket. It might have seemed like it was a coincidence to Pilates but just at that moment, John was fussing about something. "What's wrong," Pilates asked?

"When are you going to respond to Misha? I checked our e-mails and guess what? Misha, Misha, Mish, Misha."

"Alright John, I get the point."

"Do you? I check our voice mail. Misha, Misha, Misha, Misha."

"Do you think something has happen?"

"Yeah, to your head, dummy."

"I was just thinking who might want to take a trip with us overseas. Now I have my answer. If she's not too busy, Misha would love to come. I'd better call her early so she will have time to prepare for the trip."

"Hello Misha, this is Pi."

"Hello Pi. I'm so glad you called. It's been ages since I've heard your *voice*. How have you been baby?"

"I'm alright. There's a lot I want to talk to you about . . ."

"I know all about everything. That's why I have been trying to get in touch with you. If you need me for anything, just let me know. I'm here for you."

Pilates realized that Misha must have heard about his legal troubles. "Oh you heard?"

"Yes baby, I heard. It made me so angry. Who would do such a thing?"

"I haven't quite figured it out myself. I've been so busy that I haven't given it much thought."

"You haven't? They said you could get twenty years in prison if convicted Pi."

"I know this might sound a little crazy but all of it seems to pale in comparison when I think about my project."

"Pilates' Project! Is that all you can think about? People who care about you are hurting and you're talking about some project. Does your mother know about the charges?"

"I told her not to worry about it. That it was all a big mistake. Deep down inside I was hoping that it was a mistake."

"Pi, something in your *voice* is coming through the phone touching me."

"What?"

"It's hard to explain. When is the last time you talked to anyone on the phone?"

Pilates had to think on that question for a while. What kind of a question was that? Even though it was true that he had not talked on the phone for a long period of time; he didn't understand the question.

"It's been awhile alright. What is this all about?"

"Your voice sounds like my voice Pi. I know I'm talking to Pi but I hear myself talking back to me. Such a sweet voice too."

Pilates shook his head. "What's wrong with you Misha? Misha! John! John!"

"What is it Pi?"

"Something's wrong with Misha. See if you can make sense out of it."

"Hello Misha."

"Oh John, I don't know what happened. I was talking to Pi and I started getting flushed in my face and my neck. Is he alright? He didn't quite sound like himself."

"He's standing right here worried about you. He didn't know what was happening. I think he panicked and then he gave me the phone. What is it with you two? You keep putting me in the middle of things. How do you feel now?"

"I feel like I'm cooling down now. My face was burning and my neck was burning and I couldn't hear Pi. I kept hearing my own voice coming back at me like an echo. It must have been a bad connection."

"Are you on your cell," John asked?

"No, I'm on my landline phone. I was fine. I don't know what happened. Put Pi back on."

"Here you go Pi. She wants to speak to you again. She's fine now. I think she may have had a hot flash or something."

"Thanks John, she almost scared me to death. Hello Misha. Are you alright?"

Pilates thought for a moment. "Hey John, come back. I know what it is. Here, tell Misha I'm going to send her an e-mail explaining everything."

"I wish you would *explain* to me what happened. Hello Misha I'm sorry but Pilates said he was going straight to his computer to send you an e-mail immediately explaining everything. I guess the cat really did get his tongue." Misha laughed it off and thanked John. Although she thought what had happened was odd; stranger things had happened to her in her life. She couldn't wait to hear Pi's explanation on what happened.

Pilates immediately sent an e-mail to Misha.

'I'm so sorry about what happened. I guess you're tired of me talking about my upcoming project. Well, you experienced an unexpected preview of the side effects from the project. It's a little difficult to explain. I wish I could have told you beforehand but I didn't foresee that happening. It didn't dawn on me until you asked me how long it was since I had used the telephone. I have been so busy that I've actually lost track of it; but it has been a while since I've been on the phone. The reason I called you was to ask you if you'd like to go overseas with us. There's John and Peggy Lee and me. You are the odd man out. I don't think you know Peggy Lee. She's Johns' assistance (lol). He's getting so big now, he needs an assistant. Anyway, I think we were talking about my legal troubles. Don't worry about that. Let me know if you can make the trip. It will be fun! Love you, Pilates.'

After Pilates got a response back from Misha, he had John call her lawyer to set up a one hour consultation session. He wanted to get his court date postponed until after he came back from Norway.

"Good morning, I have a 10 o'clock appointment with Mr. Harold Rollins."

"Yes, Mr. Rollins is expecting you. Please go in."

"Mr. Rollins . . ."

"Are you guilty?"

"Of what?"

"Answer the question please."

"No."

"No, what?"

"No I'm not guilty."

"And why should I believe you?"

"Because the truth doesn't lie."

"Correct. Why have you made so many enemies and you're only seeking to do well? Many people have struggled with that dilemma for ages. Then they realize that the more enemies they have; the most good is being done by them. I have agreed to take your case. But if I give you alternatives to any agreements, you must weigh them in the balance as opposed to your innocence. I will never tell you to plead guilty when you're not, regardless of what is being offered. That means, this is hypothetical of course; if the judge says plead guilty and you can go free or plead innocent and you shall die; then we shall plead innocent and we shall die. What, no long face of disbelief; no face of shock? This will be the first time I've seen this. Many innocent people have come through my door and grimaced at my pithy saying. I only quote that to the people who shall receive no death sentence regardless of their innocence or guilt. The shock on their faces comes from the idea of absolute rigidity when it comes to compromise. If you think only about your personal comfort, your personal freedom then you may never know the reasons why those charges were leveled against you in the first place; but if you stand your ground, going to prison if you must; you shall know the truth and what . . ."

"The truth shall set you free."

"Correct. I believe you are innocent. I shall do my best to prove it. If I fail to succeed, then you shall see through the murky cloud of accusations, and witness the true nature of what confronts you. Leave it to me to get your court date rescheduled. I'll get it pushed back six months. I know about your awards ceremony. The fact that you are receiving that award should prove immensely valuable in the closing arguments. So go on with your life and do what you need to do but remember what I said; *truth doesn't always equal freedom.*

Pilates had six months to get his affairs in order before his trial date. That was more than enough time to go to Europe and collect his Nobel Prize and to initiate the countdown to his project. The missing formula from Switzerland should be waiting for him upon his return from Europe. Dr. Marigold was patiently waiting for the results from Dr. Moitreti. He assured Pilates that as soon as he got the results back, he would mass produce the quantities until there was more than enough for the northern hemisphere. After all, he just needed one drop of the solution per individual. The overhead cost was extremely low for such a head count. The most expensive expenditure of all was tied to the work that Dr. Moitreti was doing in Europe. However, Pilates had drained the last few dollars from his projects' account to pay for the C.E.R.N. involvement.

He was counting on his awards money to continue to fund their work after he got back from his trip. Everything now was on hold until they got back from their trip. Pilates, Misha, John and Peggy Lee took off from Charlotte Douglas International Airport en route to Oslo, Norway. After about nine hours' flight time, they landed at Oslo International airport Gardermoen. They were a day early so they decided to take in the sights and just relax. They had just completed a very strenuous year on the project without a break. Now it was time, no matter how briefly, to just take a deep breath and smell the flowers.

When Pilates was called to receive his award, he greeted the members of the committee and saluted the dignitaries and began his speech; Det är ett nöje att vara här i dag. Det är med stor ödmjukhet som jag tar emot denna utmärkelse. Jag accepterar det här priset i förväg för det arbete du ska få. När jag kommer hem ska du bära alla vittnesbörd som i inte mindre än 24 timmar skall det finnas en ny händelse i världen. Denna händelse skall börja i min hemstad Hyperion och spred sig till det bortersta hörnet av världen. Du skall inte omedelbart uppfatta någon skillnad förrän du upplever att det inte finns någon skillnad i hela mänskligheten. En värld, en själ, en röst!

TRANSLATED:

It is my pleasure to be here today. It is with great humility that I accept this award. I accept this award in advance for the work you are about to receive. When I return home, you shall all bear witness that in no less than twenty four hours, there shall be a new event in the world. This event shall start in my hometown of Hyperion and spread to the farthest corner of the globe. You shall not immediately perceive any difference until you perceive that there is no difference in all of humanity. One world, one mind, one voice!

Pilates received his medal along with thunderous applause. After a few hours mingling with the guests and other participants, Pilates and his group headed for home. After they touched down, Pilates told them to go on and get some rest. He scurried to the complex to check to see if there were any shipments. And there it was!

:To Pilates Daniels

:From Dr. Carusio Moitreti

:Care of Dr. Tom Marigold

Pilates, I have assigned these shipments to every post office in America. Per/your request/ instructions /have been also remanded/FDA approved! Injections can commence immediately.

P.S. Dr. Marigold, I hope everything works out for you!

The final stage was complete! Now all Pilates had to do was get the word out to the entire news outlets, listing the steps to be performed in the next twenty four hours. It was good that he had sent John to get some rest; he was going to need it. Pilates e-mailed this text to NASA: Operation Pilates' Project has now commenced! He checked his watch: time 12:00 am. He went to their main staging area and checked the clock: time 12:01am. Perfect. At exactly 2:00 am, Pilates woke John from his sleep and told him that it was time. John knew exactly what to do. He immediately sent out a newscast via the internet to all broadcasting stations in their area. Those same broadcasts would then recycle every thirty minutes until they would branch out to the surrounding communities and beyond. The chain reaction would engulf the entire eastern seaboard in a manner of hours. The message stated: The inoculations can commence today. Although it is not mandatory, it is highly recommended that all participate. You may suffer from delirium, tremors or even become susceptible to heart problems if you do not take the shot.

As soon as dawn broke, crowds swarmed the centers that were issuing the inoculations. Schools, post offices, hospitals and even convenience stores had supplies on hand. The product was intended for self-service. However, those who wanted assistance were told to ask for help and they would receive it. No one was to take two doses. Strict adherence to this policy was to be enforced.

A communique' was sent down the chain of command at Regional Slate Corporation that stated that none of it employees should go anywhere near the areas that were distributing the shots under the threat of termination of employment. Some of the employees actually quit their jobs in order to get the shot. But on the whole, most complied with the mandate. Likewise, some civil servants such as police, fire and the court system also refrained from receiving the shots until after a certain period had elapsed so as to keep the continuity of society flowing if something went wrong. At a precise time of the day, all four satellites initiated a pulsating signal. All of the signals were exactly the same frequency and wavelength. When one signal made contact with the other satellites, they began a slow rotation towards the surface of the earth. Each satellite was responsible for one fourth of the earths' total land mass.

At precisely the exact same hour, NASA calibrated the satellites to transmit their signal in a non-stop stream of emissions towards earth. In America, fifty percent of the population was already inoculated. Back at their complex, Pilates group began inoculating themselves. Pilates didn't take the dosage. He constantly checked on everyone else to see how they were doing. Everything appeared normal. They celebrated and high fived and took it all in with great jubilation. It was a success! Pilates was feeling good about the whole operation and momentarily forgot about his looming court date that was just around the corner. Even after the exhilarating high of his success, he still had to face the possibility of prison time.

On his court date, Pilates was punctual. His lawyer reassured him that he wouldn't let him do no more than two years in prison. Pilates thought that was better than twenty years. Regional Corporation paraded witness after witness against Pilates. Pilates was noticing something else about the whole situation. If his project was indeed a success, then how was it that the same old mundane procedures were still taking place? He knew for a fact that there was nirvana in the world somewhere, but here he was, stuck in this place, listening to these crazy testimonies. He wanted to be outside in communion with the stillness but instead he was trapped inside commingled with all the deflating noise. Finally the prosecutor called Director Richard Thornton. Pilates refocused on him to see exactly what this whole farce was all about. The prosecutor asked the director questions with the tone of his voice sounding amicable and restive.

"Director Thornton; tell us in your own words what happened that day when the defendant visited your establishment."

"Well, he seemed like a nice young man. I offered him a job. He refused the . . ."

"Wait. I won't the court to hear this. He refused the job?"

"That's right. I told him he was what we were looking for in an applicant. I told him he had already passed the exams. He said he wanted his own office. He said he wanted an independent study. He said he wanted a place where he didn't have to worry about testing his employees or anyone for that matter. Actually I began to fear for my life. I told the applicant that he would have to leave. I told him that if he didn't want to finalize the deal of getting the job, then he would have to leave. He got loud and boisterous and threatened me. I told him I would have to call security. He said he was leaving then. I didn't feel like I had any reason to follow him to make sure he was leaving so I went on about my daily routine. It was a little while after he left my office, that a staffer told me that he saw Mr. Daniels go upstairs instead of downstairs. Important papers were missing the next day. Trade secrets we normally keep away from competitors were gone. Let me say this, we are in the business of communication. We don't try to outdo our competitors. We believe in helping and sharing with everyone. With that said, we do have trade secrets. Every specialized corporation has them. The thing about trade secrets is; once they are stolen, your company isn't specialized any more. You are then a wide open company with no identity and no community. He took our identity and he took our namesake!

Pilates rubbed his head and thought, what a lie!

Thornton nose suddenly burst open into a bloody stream as if someone had struck him. Thornton calmly got his handkerchief out and staunched the flow of blood. He then straightened his necktie and thought, 'go to hell'.

Pilates looked down at his ankle and it looked as if it had been burnt in a furnace. He rolled his sock down below the burnt mark to let some air hit the spot. Pilates thought: one world, one mind, one voice.

He looked up and to his surprise, he saw Thornton getting up out of the witness box. The judge said, "They haven't finished questioning you yet. Sit back down!"

Thornton kept walking as if he was in a daze. His attorney quickly spoke up and said, "Your honor, my client isn't feeling very well today. He already has a ruptured sinus. He's trying to give all the facts. He told me before the trial began that he was not feeling very well."

"Alright, you may step down. Counselor, next time don't put an infirmed client on my witness stand."

"Yes your honor."

"Thornton continued to walk out of the courtroom oblivious to his surroundings. Pilates thought, what in the world is wrong with him. He looked zombified. Pilates looked down at his ankle and wondered how it got burned so badly while he was just sitting there. It was aching a lot too. He whispered to his attorney that he needed a break. Rollins nodded and proceeded to engage the judge. "Your honor, can we have a fifteen minutes recess?"

"Fifteen minutes it is!"

"Pilates told Rollins he didn't like to complain but that he was in a great deal of pain. He said he needed some balm or aloe to soothe his leg. Rollins asked him what had happened and Pilates wasn't able to explain it. He said it burned like fire. Rollins went out and got the attention of a bailiff and they secured a first aid kit. He found some ointment and hurried back to the men's room. Pilates put all of the ointment on the burn. It felt soothing with each layer until all of the ointment was gone. "Are you ready?"

"I believe so," Pilates replied.

They headed back into the courtroom without mentioning the bizarre behavior of Richard Thornton. Pilates wanted Rollins to call Thornton back to the witness stand but, Rollins explained to Pilates that before the nosebleed and the blanking out episode, Thornton had the jury mesmerized; they were literally hanging onto his every word. He told Pilates that he was glad Thornton got sick on the stand; because if he had stayed up there a little longer, he didn't believe that he would have been able to refute any of Thornton's testimony. Rollins, instead, called the staffer Robert Higgins to the stand.

"Robert Higgins."

"Bob, please."

"Bob. You gave a statement, testifying that you noticed Mr. Daniels going upstairs instead of downstairs. Why is that?"

"I beg your pardon."

"Why did you notice my client at all?"

"I, ugh, I . . ."

"You didn't notice him did you? You have never seen my client before today. Even if what you say is true; why would you go to the directors' office and report that a man was going upstairs instead of going downstairs?"

"For security rea . . ."

"If it was for security, you would have alerted the security guards. They would have handled the situation, not the Director. My client would have had the time to do all those things that you said he did while you were bypassing security, going to the directors' office to tell him about the incident so that he could call security. Is that your companies' protocol? If anything happens, go directly to the Directors' office, so he can get security, so they can then stop whatever's going on?"

"Objection your honor."

"On what grounds?"

"He's leading my witness. He's putting words in his mouth."

"Counselor, let the witness respond to the question."

"Yes your honor. Mr. Higgins or shall I say Bob? What exactly do you do for the company?

"I, ugh, I . . ."

"Your honor, I don't want to put words in the witness mouth but I feel the need to fill in the gaps that the witness is leaving out."

"By all means, do, the judge replied."

"Since you hesitated to state your occupation, I'll create one for you. You are a paid staffer. Your job is to say whatever you are told to say. That's it. End of job description."

"Objection your honor."

"That's alright. I have no further questions."

"Plaintiff."

"No questions your honor. We would like to call Pilates Daniels."

"You may step down."

"Pilates Daniels, please come forward."

"Pilates Daniels. Do you have a Ph.D.?"

"No sir, I don't."

"Do you have a Masters'?"

"No sir."

"A bachelors'?"

"No sir."

"What do you have?"

"An Associate Degree."

"I see. Good for you. How is it that you can speak so many languages all of a sudden?"

"I'm waiting on the doctors and the scientists to tell me that."

"Ha Ha Ha! That's a good one. Really, you can't even speak two languages now can you? No. Don't answer that. Answer this. Say good morning in Chinese."

"Why?"

"Because, you broke into the Regional Slate Institute Corporation. You stole their methods and you duped a lot of people into believing some mumbo jumbo crap about a universal language didn't you?"

"Objection your honor!"

"On what grounds?"

"We have a linguist in the courtroom. Can he come forward?"

"Please do!"

"菲利普."

"What did my client say?" asked attorney Rollins.

"He called my name."

"Have you ever met my client?"

"No."

"What is your name?"

"Philip."

"Talk to him Philip."

The jury listened and heard Chinese being spoken until they heard something else. Each member of the jury leaned forward because there was something familiar about the speech, but yet, they had never heard it spoken before.

The linguist was trembling because he understood what was being said but he didn't understand how he understood.

Pilates cried. It wasn't supposed to be like this. He saw some, not much, but he saw some of the fruits of his labor. He just wished that they would get on with it and give him his sentence so all of this torture could be over with.

After a day of summation, the two sides rested their case. The jury came back with a guilty plea but with the stipulation that there was no sabotage. They concluded that there was no theft. They found Pilates guilty of intellectual property tampering by interfering with trade secrets of the Regional Institute. They agreed with the prosecution that Pilates must have come across some of the secrets of the Corporation; because how else could he have acquired such a mastery of so many languages in such a short period of time that even a linguistic expert trembled before him?

The Judge was now ready to pronounce sentencing. He spoke directly to Pilates.

"In light of all the extenuating circumstances, I'm not going to give you what the verdict require. You have no past criminal record. You have just won the most prestigious award in the world. You have accomplished what only a very few can comprehend and yet, you have done it at such a young age. But the law is the law. The requirement for being guilty on one account is two years. However, in your case, I am cutting it to one year to be served and one year of probation with the possibility of parole in six months."

Harold Rollins hugged Pilates and stopped and said," do you remember what we discussed? Keep focus."

"Pilates had almost forgotten what Rollins had told him because it was such an emotional day for him. He started to focus in on the reason he was charged in the first place. And it was just as Rollins had said; Thornton really did have something to hide. Pilates made a mental note that he would investigate the secret that Regional Institute was trying so desperately to keep, once he got out of prison. He couldn't complain about the verdict. He was looking at two years, but now with a little luck, he may be free in six months.

The court gave Pilates a week to get his affairs in order before he was to report to prison to serve his sentence. He handed over the reins of the operation to John and Peggy. He said good bye to his staff. They had about twenty five people in their group who were loyal to Pilates and they had worked diligently to help him get the project off the ground. They could see the kernels of the project slowly moving one cog at a time. It was only a matter of time now before at least ninety five percent of the earth's population would be rapturously intertwine in one world, one mind, and one voice.

Pilates tried to keep to himself while he was on the inside but he knew he had to assemble and mingle with the populace or else, he would surely be singled out by the other inmates. He wasn't assigned to a maximum security prison but he felt that a prison was still a prison. He tried to make the most of his time by reading but his mind always wandered. He wondered why the inmates hadn't received their injections. They were the prime group who should have received it. He had to remember once he got out, to list prisons for the shipment of the dosages.

Three months had passed and Pilates had settled into the prison routine. One day while he was looking at the television set in the recreation area, he noticed that it continually displayed wavy lines. He knew about poor reception in older model televisions so he asked if he could look at it to see if he could repair it. The guard told him he'd have to get back to him on that after he had run it by his superiors. Pilates understood and said fine. However, while Pilates was in the rec area, he heard the voices on the screen; the picture was so fuzzy he couldn't see them; he heard the voices say: 'Tomorrow will be a make it or break it day for us. If we can make it through the intense solar flares without total mishap then we'll be alright.' Pilates panicked! Solar flares! The newscaster continued on: 'Try not to use any electrical appliances unless you absolutely have to, such as in an emergency situation. We know in this day and age it's very difficult to do but; cut off all your computers for the day, and take them out of their surge protectors. Disconnect TVs. You may want to keep a small transistor radio to listen to for emergency broadcasts. Above all, stay inside. These solar flares are going to be the most intense solar activity in our earths' history, so please be very careful.'

Pilates rushed to the front desk and ask for permission to use the computer. "Daniels, you know the rules. You can use the phone. No computers.'

Pilates moaned in his spirit. He remembered what happened the last time he tried to talk on the phone to Misha. Should he try to test it out again. No, he reasoned to himself, it was too dangerous. They had taken the dosage and he didn't know how they would respond to his voice over the phone.

They were watching the same news that he was seeing. Surely someone would come to check with him about the situation, he thought. But he knew they probably wouldn't ever arrive in time. Damage from intense solar flares was the one thing that Pilates had not anticipated in his rush to get his project off the ground! He didn't know what effect the flares would have on the satellites. If the satellites went down, the people who had taken the dosage would probably be alright but those who didn't take the dosage would probably go stark raving mad. Pilates thought: *and it would all be my fault.* If he broke into the computer room, they would hike his time back up to two full years. With all of his worrying about the world on the outside, Pilates didn't stop to contemplate about what would happen to him while he was trapped there on the inside with the prisoners. It was all panning out to be a real nightmare for Pilates.

Pilates went to bed but he didn't go to sleep. He lay awake all night long hoping that when the dawn of a new day peered through the windows, the sunlight would vanquish all of his problems along with the night. Pilates awoke to the sound of a cock crowing remotely in the distance. He immediately noticed all of the inmates missing from their cots. He hadn't slept a wink all night, or so he thought. He wondered how they could have arisen without his knowledge. He must have fallen asleep sometime during the night. He hurriedly threw on some trousers and a khaki shirt and headed outside into the courtside. What he saw next was a chilling sight to behold. The inmates were all standing in a lineal straight line, their bodies rigidly still, facing the eastern gate. Pilates cocked his head to one side as he tried to understand what this meant. It was 7:00 in the morning and already the temperature felt like it was approaching one hundred degrees. Pilates didn't want to get too close to the inmates because he didn't know what to expect from them. He found a shady spot in a corner and sat down and observed the inmates. They stood motionless for two hours in the scorching sun.

Pilates noticed that none of them seemed to break a sweat. He thought it was odd because his clothes were now completely drenched with perspiration. He went inside and found the water faucet and sipped the water for about thirty minutes. He wondered where the administrative staff had gone. He peeked around the corner to find them also hovering in some kind of catatonic state. If they breathed at all, it was so shallow that it was undetectable by the unaided human eye. Did the solar flares produce this? He thought the flares would cause an opposite reaction from the situation than what he was now witnessing. He had to escape! He didn't want to be left in there at night with these creepy zombie like inmates. He was thinking that he only had three more months to go before he was scheduled to be released. If he escape, they may give him the full term now. They should understand why he just had to get out of there though.

Pilates walked all around the encampment to be doubly sure there were no animated guards around. If there were any and they saw him; he knew he'd be in hot water. They may even hurt him for trying to escape. Pilates hollered out: 'Help', until he was hoarse. Since no one came to his rescue, Pilates made up his mind to scale the barbed wire fence to freedom. He knew it was a tricky thing to do. Unlike in the movies when the jailbreak is a success, Pilates was well aware of the dangers he faced from lethally injuring himself by getting entangled in the wires to the point where he couldn't break free. With no one around to hear him scream, he could easily bleed to death. He had to be methodical in his approach; he must cover every angle. Pilates also knew that he might not have that much time before the inmates were revived. Who knew what state of minds they were going to be in when they did come to. Pilates wasn't sticking around to find out. He began to climb. It took some maneuvering and positioning but Pilates made it over without getting cut. The *razor* sharp barbed wire wasn't as difficult to cross when time stood still and allowed him to pass over at his own deliberate pace. Climbing down the fence, Pilates' face was now very close to some of the inmates' faces, with only the metal fence separating them. He could see the vacuous stare in their eyes up close. When he was finally all the way down on the ground; Pilates began to cry at the sight of the men standing before him on the other side of the fence. Why were they all standing so starkly still in that straight line, facing outward, he wondered? All of this, the entire situation, he felt; was nobody else's fault but his alone. He stood in the hot noon day sun for one full hour, just staring at the inmates, to see if they would eventually move; hoping intensely that they would move, because it looked as if they would most certainly die from the scorching heat if they continued to stand motionless outside all day long. Pilates felt himself getting dehydrated so he slowly turned and wiped a tear from his eye and ran across the *plains* as fast as he could to escape.

A fugitive on the run, the status of his project uncertain; Pilates didn't know where to begin. They may have very well already put out an All-Points Bulletin on him. He had to keep that fact in consideration until he contacted the proper authorities and explained to them what had happened. The fact that he escaped; even though it was from a minimum security prison, worried Pilates a great deal. He knew he was going to turn himself in the first chance he got but, would that be enough to satisfy the authorities and help him avoid all the repercussions that come from being a fugitive from justice? He hated what he had done but felt he had no choice. He prepared for the worse. He took all the isolated roads so that he wouldn't draw any undue attention to himself and he stayed off the highways, even though the highway was the quickest route home. He had no money, food or water; and on top of all that; he was traveling on foot with the temperatures soaring now higher than they ever had been before.

Tired, dehydrated and famished, Pilates saw he was almost home; he had been walking for four hours. Pilates mumbled to himself that if he had used the highway, he would have been home even sooner; nonetheless, he felt that he could make it; the nearer he got to home. He had about thirty more minutes or so to walk before he reached his destination. Pilates wondered why he had not seen anyone since his escape. He picked up the pace; he wanted to get home before it got dark. Remembering that he had set his home alarm when he went away, and he didn't have any keys to get in; to break a window, trigger an alarm and cause the police to come out without their knowing about his situation was not an option for Pilates. He figured he should go to Johns' house first and regroup from there. It was about 5:00 in the evening but Pilates didn't know what time it was. He didn't have his watch. He needed to know the time because he could then estimate whether John had left the Project complex building for the day. John rarely stayed late because he didn't have to. Pilates wasn't so sure about whether John would stay late or not today because it was an unprecedented day. He had to get more information about what was going on. Up until now it had all been speculation and guesses. It was time to get the facts.

"Hello. Hello. Anybody home?" Pilates got no answer so he hid himself so no one could see that he was there. He waited. It was about an hour later when John pulled into his driveway. Pilates had fallen asleep. Weakened from the long walk and the heat and humidity, Pilates was severely dehydrated now. John went inside unaware of Pilates' presence since he was partially hidden from view behind the shrubbery in his back yard. Around midnight Pilates began talking out of his head; deliriously rambling on and on. First he spoke in one language and then he spoke in another. His ramblings went on and on until he sat up and looked around to gather his bearings. He noticed that it was very late and that he had fallen asleep. He knocked on Johns' door until a small light turned on.

"Who is it?"

"John, it's me, Pilates. Please let me in!" John slowly opened the door and saw a gaunt looking Pilates, weary worn and desperate. "What in the world are you doing here Pi? What happened? How did you get here?" Pilates was so weak he couldn't seem to generate enough energy to talk. John caught him before he fell and brought him inside. He raced to his refrigerator and got a bottle of water. Pilates snatched

the bottle from his hands and gulped in long swallowing motions until the bottle was completely empty. It took about thirty seconds. *"More! More!"* John went back and got the whole pack of water. There were five remaining bottles. Pilates swallowed them all in about five minutes. He tried to get more but John told him to wait a few minutes. There was a crazed look in Pilates' eyes. He now knew that he had seen something that he might not ever be able to explain to anyone. John rushed to his phone and called Dr. Marigold. "Hello doctor. This is John Palley. Yes. I really am sorry to call you at this hour but this is an emergency. I know, but I'm talking about Pilates. That's right. He's here with me. I know but . . . something happened. No he hasn't told me what it is yet. He appears dehydrated for one thing. There seems to be a whole lot wrong with him. He looks like he's in shock too. I don't know how he got here. I've been home since 6:30. I didn't see him when I came in. He's resting now. I need to know if I should try to give him something to eat. Alright. How long? I'll be waiting. No I haven't. I won't."

John was thinking that the doctor was very paranoid about something. He said he shouldn't take longer than forty-five minutes to get there. Dr. Marigold told John to give Pilates a few teaspoons of broth and keep him well ventilated until he got there. He said it sounded like Pilates was suffering from heat exhaustion but he couldn't know for sure until he examined him. John paced backed and forth in a circle. It was the look on Pilates' face that frightened John. He had never seen Pilates face look like that before.

He wished the doctor would hurry because something else could be wrong with Pilates. After the doctor arrived, John sighed loudly, as if a big burden was lifted from his shoulder. The doctor immediately ran a series of tests. He got back to John saying, "you were right. He's severely dehydrated with heat exhaustion and shock." The doctor explained that the shock might be twofold; meaning that, Pilates not only was in shock from the heat; but there was something else that was disturbing him as well. John agreed. He said he thought the same thing. "Can you let him rest here tonight?"

"Sure. He can stay here as long as necessary."

"Good. He should be fine after you give him some of these pills tomorrow. Keep his diet fluid for a couple of days and let me know when he is ready to talk. I want to hear what he has to say."

"Me too doctor. Me too."

When Pilates awoke, he thought he had just come out of a very bad nightmarish dream until he looked around and saw that he wasn't at the camp anymore. He gradually began to remember bits and pieces of what had happened to him. He quickly stood up but nearly keeled over from the blood rushing to his head. His head felt light as a feather so he immediately sat back down on the bed for a few moments to get his equilibrium back in balance. He wanted to talk to John and find out what was going on with the project. He called out to John; but he noticed his voice was so raspy from screaming so much back at the yard that he could barely hear himself talk. *Laryngitis!*

"Morning Pi. How're you doing today? What's wrong?" Pilates motioned to his mouth and shook his head. "You lost your voice? How did you lose your voice?" Pilates felt lower that he had felt for quite some time. Here he was a Nobel Prize winner with a mammoth project that allowed the world to fully understand one another with a universal language and he couldn't even communicate with John about what had happened to him. He motioned for paper and pen. He wrote: What about solar flares? Are they gone? Did anything strange happen? Is everybody alright?

John looked at Pilates very hard, trying his best to figure out what Pilates was trying to say. He responded to the questions. "Pi, we heard about the solar flares. They say the same thing every year, don't they? According to the weatherman, the flares should stick around for a while. He quoted a term, one solar year. As for anything strange happening, I can't say. I haven't noticed anything strange until I saw you tonight. What are you doing here Pi? How did you get out?"

Pilates wrote: I escaped!

John became livid. "What! Escape! Who in their right mind would escape with three months to go in a minimum security lock up? I'm sorry Pi; I just don't understand. We need you back for the project. You risk going back to prison for two years!" John saw that he was making Pilates very depressed and eased back a little? "Why Pi? Why?" Pilates wrote: I was afraid. Then Pilates wrote in bold letters: SOMEONE NEEDS TO GO TO THE CAMP AND GET THOSE INMATES INSIDE. THEY'RE PROBABLY NEAR DEATH. CALL SOMEONE UP THERE TO SEE IF THEY ARE ALRIGHT. IF NO ANSWERS GET MARIGOLD TO GO. IT'S BEEN A VERY LONG TIME NOW SINCE I LEFT THEM. HURRY!

"Alright! I'm calling now. There's no answer at the camp. Shouldn't we just notify someone up there? It'll take us a few hours to get there." Pilates shook his head no. John assembled some of the Project group members together and got Dr. Marigold to go. They left Pilates behind at Johns' house until they could figure out what was going on at the camp. When they got to the camp, they found it to be just as Pilates had described it. The inmates appeared to be in some sort of suspended animation. They let the youngest and most athletic of the group climb over the fence to get in. He placed two blankets over the barbed wire fence and dropped down inside quite easily. He then opened the door to the camp from the inside, letting everyone in. Dr. Marigold immediately raced up and down the line checking the inmates' vital signs. He got a pulse from all of them but he didn't get any other kind of reaction from them at all. They immediately took the inmates inside one at a time and laid them on their cots. Dr. Marigold laid cold compresses on their heads and made makeshift intravenous tubes beside each of their cots. They did the same for the administrative personnel and the security guards. They found it hard to come up with an explanation to explain this event.

Dr. Marigold was becoming quite concerned that they were getting into a legal dilemma with their actions at the camp. He said Pilates needed to get back to the camp as quickly as possible and that they should notify the proper authorities without delay about the situation as soon as possible because they had no way to explain their involvement at the camp. He even went so far as to joke that they may have to get a cot of their own and check in at the camp with Pilates. None of the group was amused. They agreed to leave some behind while the others went back to get Pilates. The plan was to get Pilates back before anyone even knew he had ever left. It was going to be night before they got back from the round trip. Dr. Marigold reluctantly stayed because he had to monitor the inmates' immediate conditions but he had certain qualms about being left inside the camp unauthorized for such a long period of time. There were going to be questions asked. John and Peggy Lee went back to Hyperion to get Pilates while Stanley Broom, George Carson, Jill Solares and Sara Vaughn stayed with the doctor.

John was hurrying as fast and as safe as he could to get to Pilates. He wished Pilates had gone back with them in the first place. But in the back of his mind; there was this sinking feeling of not wanting to leave Pilates at the camp alone unattended with those inmates. If the doctor said he couldn't explain what happened there, then why should they leave Pilates all alone, as if nothing had happened at all? One or two of the group should remain with Pilates until reinforcement came to set everything back in proper alignment.

When they got back to Pilates, John told him that everything he had said was true. He told him the doctor wanted him back before they alerted the authorities to protect him. John saw that Pilates was a little nervous about going back. He told Pilates that if it came down to that, they all would stay with him until the proper personnel came. Pilates relented and soon they were on their way back to the camp. It was growing dark now and Pilates was becoming increasingly nervous because he had lost his voice. He took that as a bad omen even though he didn't believe in such things.

They finally reached the camp. Pilates felt a little better now because he had witnesses to testify on his behalf if it ever had to come down to that. When they entered the camp, Pilates heard John call out to Dr. Marigold; but he didn't get an answer back in return. They couldn't find anyone else inside either. All the inmates were gone! John called Peggy Lee and told her to stay close. He told Pilates to stay where he could see him since he was unable to speak. Pilates had the same crushing sensation he had yesterday morning when he first got out of bed. Even with John and Peggy Lee with him, he still felt haplessly alone. When they walked around to the other side of the camp, they saw in the darkness, the eerie stillness of silhouetted figures, standing in a perfect lineal line facing the western gate. The doctor and the rest of the group could not be found. Pilates tugged on Johns' shirt, indicating that he wanted to leave. John said, "Pi, we can't just leave without knowing where they've gone. Something is going on here, and if we don't figure it out soon, they'll blame it all on you just like they blame the other thing on you. You shouldn't even have been here in the first place."

When Pilates lost his voice, he lost a little piece of his vision, of what he was trying to accomplish in the world. His mantra had become: One world, one mind and one voice, but now with his voice gone, a little something else was taken out of him, something like faith and courage. All he knew was; he wanted to leave and he wanted to leave right then. But this time was different now than it was before; before, he had to escape because he was alone. Now he had to wait, good or bad; he had to wait because he was not alone. It was almost eleven o'clock and John was desperately trying to locate the five members of the group that were left behind. Pilates hurriedly scribbled: John, you need to call the authorities now. It's about more than me now. Let them know what's going on here. Something bad may have happened to them. We just don't know.

John got on the phone. "Hello. Highway Patrol. We're at Sidney Green Correctional facility. Something is wrong here. My name is John Palley. We were guests but five of our party members have gone missing. We were visiting a friend. Yes our friend is alright. He's still here except he has lost his voice. That's right. He can't speak. We're very confident it's only temporary. Can you send some people over here? Can we wait outside for them? The inmates are still inside but there's something wrong with them. I can't explain it; you have to see it for yourself. We'll be outside a few blocks away. The gate can't be locked from the outside. There is no security here. I don't know. I don't know. Can we leave? Something is wrong here! I don't know. He can't talk."

Pilates stood there just looking at John; precious time was wasting. They needed to leave before whatever happened to Doctor Marigold and the rest of the group happened to them. Pilates wondered why the person on the other end of the line was so concerned about him. He wanted to scream but he couldn't. John grabbed Peggy Lee's hand and said they should leave. They left the camp and headed to the parking lot; got into their car and pulled away from the area about a few hundred yards and waited. It was now approaching midnight. John and Peggy Lee were trying very hard to figure out what was the best course of action that they should take. They decided that they should wait a little longer for the highway patrol to arrive.

"John, look! What is that," Peggy shrieked? John turned around and saw a faint splatter of sunlight glimmering with sporadic waves of movement peeking over the horizon. He traced the sunlit rays from their source to the encamped prison area. There were the inmates, outside the fence, encircling it!

Through the eerie darkness, John saw through the miniscule rays, a beacon of sunlight illuminate the eyes of the men outside the gate. Instead of blank listless faces, there were now glowing defined visages of emanating light. They marched around the camp with their steps synchronized to precision. The pace was hauntingly slow. Each step they took seemed like an eternity. "I don't know what to make of it," John said.

"How did they get outside without us knowing it? Why are they barely moving? Where is all that dust coming from?" John had no answer. He heard screaming and yelling but didn't know where it was coming from until he heard familiar voices calling to them. "We're over here!"

"No, we're over here!" John got out and looked peeringly across the plains through the dust and darkness and saw Stanley and George. "Stanley, George, where have y'all been? We've been worried sick about y'all. Where are the others?"

"We got separated somehow," said George.

"It was very strange," Stanley added.

"Help!"

"Who's there," cried Stanley?

"It's us. Where are you," Jill and Sara alternated saying?

Stanley, George and John branched off into the darkness a little more and came back with Jill and Sara.

"What happened," Sara asked?

"We don't know," George replied.

"Where's Dr. Marigold," John asked?

"He left earlier. He got very nervous after y'all left. He said it was highly improper for him to be here. He put Stanley in charge and told us that the inmates' conditions were stabilized," George explained.

"But where did he say he was going?"

"Back home."

"I made a call to the highway patrol. I gave them my name. I reported you all missing. It's going to be almost impossible to explain this now! What am I supposed to say," John asked?

"How are the inmates," asked Stanley?

"Can't you see . . ." John said, pointing to the camp? To John's surprise, the inmates were gone.

"Where did they go," John pleaded?

"What do you mean John," George asked?

"I mean just a few seconds ago, they were marching around the camp very, very slowly and now they're gone."

"I thought we placed everyone on their beds inside the prison, screamed Sara!"

"We did but . . ." John grew tired of trying to rationalize the irrational. "Let's go," he said.

"Great," George offered.

"Fine by me," added Stanley. The women nodded. They got into their cars and left the camp parking lot. Pilates remained with the group. By now he had fallen asleep, totally exhausted from the frenzied excitement of the last two days.

The next morning Pilates awoke with renewed strength and extra vigor. He had missed a lot of the strange happenings from last night. He didn't even know that Stanley, George, Sara and Jill had returned with them from the correctional facility until John told him the entire story about what had transpired. Pilates wanted to go home and sleep in his own bed. He was grateful that John had helped him out by letting him stay a couple of days but he didn't want to intrude on Johns' personal life. He had made up his mind that he wasn't going back to the camp. He was just going to have to be a fugitive. John told him that they were going to have to figure out all of the necessary prerequisites before they could do a simple thing like get him back into his house. Pilates had regained his voice now and talked more forceful than ever. He told John to take him home and he would show him the simple prerequisite for getting in. John consented and took Pilates home and watched to his dismay as Pilates picked up a rather large sized brick and tossed it through his window. The blaring of the alarm caused John to shrink down in his car seat while Pilates boldly strode inside and calmly answered his alarm and told security everything was 'AOK'. John shook his head at how easy Pilates had made it seem; knowing that it wasn't very easy at all.

Pilates laid out a new strategy to his group. He said before the project could be one hundred percent effective, he had to investigate Regional Slate Institute. He told them that he had notice during his trial that something peculiar was going on at their establishment. He didn't know if it was the solar flares or the secrets they kept; he only knew something was interfering with their project and he had to find out what it was. He stressed to them that it had to be a one man's job. They were to say that they knew nothing of his plans if he were ever caught during any of his investigations. Pilates thanked each and every member for their hard work and dedication to the project. He said that he would very much like to give a special thanks to Stanley, George, Sara, Jill, Peggy Lee and John.

It was amazing that no one looked backed or asked questions about the events that took place at the correctional facility. Pilates wasn't worried anymore about his fugitive status. He had a focus now that seemed other worldly as he set out to find the whereabouts of Richard Thornton and decode any secrets that Thornton had tried to cover up. The first place to logically look was at Thornton's home base. He went to Regional Slate Institute and entered the establishment; only this time he entered under false pretenses. He asked to see the director in person concerning a charitable donation that he wanted to bestow upon the corporation. When he was told that the director had taken a leave of absence, he mumbled about his gift being too large to just leave at the desk. He said he wanted to present the endowment officially to Mr. Thornton in person. Pilates was told to go upstairs and wait while the staffer tried to find Thornton's assistant. Pilates thanked the staffer and proceeded to head towards the stairwell until he glanced back and saw that the staffer had left the desk. Pilates then ran behind the desk to look up personnel offices and specific room numbers. He was curious as to why the basement was labeled SLATE. Instead of taking the elevator down which was faster, Pilates took to the stairwell. He was almost to the basement which was a total of five flights of stairs down; when he quickly stopped after glimpsing armed security personnel patrolling the corridors below. He tried a head count but that proved to be somewhat of a tricky task. There were two guards at the desk. Two more were on the right wing while two others oversaw the left wing. But Pilates knew he couldn't be sure about the exact number that was just beyond that door on the other side of it. He felt consternation at the fact that there were so many armed men patrolling such a small area. What could it be on the other side of that door that warranted such attention with such manpower? But of course, that was the primary reason he was there, to find out why. Suddenly Pilates heard footsteps descending the stairs with muffled voices as he scrambled to hide himself. After the floor that he was on, there were no obstacles insight that he could use as cover or a barrier between himself and the guards.

He hid behind an oval shaped ashtray that stood about four feet off the floor. He squatted as low as his body would allow him to go. The two men walked past him deeply engaged in a spirited conversation. He heard one man mention a slate while the other man appeared highly enamored with the broached subject. Pilates wondered what was so interesting about what they were saying that once they reached the desk; they felt the need to halt their conversation completely and switch to a more triteness in their speech.

When the door to the north corridor swung open, Pilates caught sight of an enormous vault shimmering in the vacant room; revealing a composite mix of chromium tensiled plated stainless steel, galvanized with huge metallic cables connecting each side of the vault to its' door. He caught only a glimpse of the vault's door opening when the two men entered the room. He surmised that the vaults' security mechanism must have automatically engaged once the two men entered the room. He checked his watch. It was exactly 4:30 pm. He had a hunch that the Regional Corporation probably would never actually shut down its business, so he plotted a scheme to stay in the corner where he was until the shift change; and then make his move when more of the staffers entered the vault room. The security cameras could not scan his position, because as long as he remained absolutely still; he could go undetected for a long period of time.

At 5:00 pm, the shift change was scheduled to occur. Pilates could tell the exact time the two shifts were exchanging places with one another by all the bustling and the din of the crowd that was entering and exiting the building upstairs. There were now only two armed guards present near the desk. While the guards were waiting on their replacements, two members of the council came downstairs and entered the vault. Before the guards could even look his way, Pilates was up and running and had made it into the room cleanly behind the two men without being seen. With a strong jab of his fist, Pilates landed a blow to the back of the head of one of the men just above the nape of his neck. He proceeded with a full uppercut to the jaw of the other employee, leaving them both temporarily unconscious. The door to the vault was now wide open as if some biometric scanner sensing device had detected the men and prompted an automatic sequence to initiate, thereby allowing Pilates entry into the vault. Pilates scooped up the case with the enclosed sliver of metal that was on a stand in the middle of the vault; placed it in his pocket and walked casually up the stairs as if he were an employee of the company. He flowed with the outgoing traffic of the exiting shift until he was completely blocked from the view of the screens that the Institute guards were monitoring. After surveying the area around him to see if he was followed or not, Pilates saw that he had gotten away undetected. He raced home with a great deal of alacrity so that he could fully examine the mysterious artifact in detail. He had gone to great lengths to get the object and he wasn't about to give it up until he had deciphered the truth behind it.

Saul Chambers, the assistant director of Regional Slate Institute, upon being notified of the break-in and theft of the SLATE, called a special session for the council to meet. The names of the other council members in attendance were: Henry Wilkins, Thomas Applecott, William Delphino, Jude Gibbons, Herman Shaw, Joseph Taylor, Herbert Trefant, Donald Sinclair, Tim Tobias and Theodore Roberts.

"Gentlemen I called this special session because as you all are aware; the SLATE has been stolen!" All of the members held their heads in disbelief as barely noticeable moans of exasperation were circulating around the room. "I have procured the services of some special private detectives to help us retrieve the SLATE. It will probably be only a matter of weeks before it is in our possession again. I have also asked them to find the whereabouts of Richard Thornton who you know disappeared so suddenly without a trace. The local authorities have had no success with any leads in finding him. We have tried to keep his disappearance as confidential as we possibly could so as not to upset our investment board members. But we need him now more than we ever did before. We shall be suspending our operations in the meantime and report to the press that we have to lay off some of our employees worldwide. This may cause some confusion at first but I don't foresee any questions arising that we are unable to answer, unless the person who has stolen the SLATE, knows the true value and power of the artifact which he has in his possession. Only if he goes public, shall we be in ruins."

"Saul, who do you think took it," asked William Delphino?

"I don't know, but if Richard were here, I am very sure that he would have had the names already. I am sorry that I am not as astute concerning the SLATE as he is. However, he has named me number 2, and so I shall try to the best of my ability to commune with the president of the company, who we all know wishes to remain anonymous to us. I have not tried nor will I try to ascertain his identity, although it would be a great deal easier for us if we knew who he was."

"But Saul, how are we to go about our business without the SLATE, even if it's just gone for a week," Thomas Applecott inquired?

"Thomas, we have to shut down all of our activities because even though we can wing it for a while; there is too much risk in exposing ourselves to the world concerning the power of the SLATE."

Tim Tobias asked a question that made the entire council become more reflective when he said, "what are we supposed to do now?"

Saul slowly answered Tobias and said, "nothing. We shall all go somewhere and wait. We shall answer no questions from the press nor shall we be seen in public. I have accessed the emergency fund for precisely this purpose. I will give each member a certain amount of money on their company card to be used during this period of uncertainty. Henry Wilkins shall make note in his ledger the amount and the total appropriation of funds accessed. He shall then make note of how long the period lasts. If the period lasts for longer that one month, Henry shall then make accessible the exact same amount to all of you until this matter is closed. Where you go is not important; each of you shall have a choice on that decision. You are to make certain that wherever you do go; you will not be seen as representatives of this company.

The members all agreed to the consensus of the vote that was taken and slowly filed out of the room, not knowing what to expect now that the power of the SLATE had been taken from them.

Pilates called a meeting of his group. He told them to meet him at his home in order to keep it confidential. He also invited Dr. Marigold. When they all arrived at his home, they were bursting with curiosity over what he had found out about the corporation.

"Listen, I found this small piece of metal in the Regional Slate Corporation building."

"What is it, and why is it so important to us," asked Stan?

"I don't know what it is. I don't know if it is important to us. But what I do know is; it was very important to them. I know that it must be something their entire company needs in order for them to function and stay in business."

"Then why did you bring it here; and why did you get us involved with it? Surely they are going to be looking all over for that thing. They are probably at this very moment offering a huge reward to anybody with information concerning it," shouted George.

"No," explained Pilates. "I think they are going to hire someone private to look for it. They are not going to the police this time about it. You won't hear about this on the news or see a reward offer."

"And how do you know that," asked Jill?

"I know this to be a fact because; I never applied to that company for any kind of grant. I didn't fully realize it at the time, but their company isn't in the business of giving away grants. This thing is to them so top secret, that they must have felt threatened by something I did or by something that I said. It may have been because of my project. At any rate, they framed me to get me out of the picture. My lawyer was very good though. They wanted to send me away for twenty years. They might have succeeded too, had Thornton not gotten sick on the stand.

Harold Rollins told me to beware of him. He said Thornton had the power of persuasion. If Thornton got his power from this little trinket; that would be really amazing, wouldn't it?"

The doctor picked up the small piece of medal and summed up, "it really does seem ridiculous for us to pay such attention to such a small object. Why do you think it is so valuable Pilates?"

"They guarded it like it was fort Knox or something. You wouldn't believe the manpower they had overseeing this thing. The vault that contained it looked as if it was built to hold something else. I mean, it was so huge and the only item that was on the inside of it was this small trinket. Doctor, I need to know what type of metal it is; I need to know its basic structure and the purpose that it could be used for. Obviously, we don't want to send it off for study so; how can we fully understand what type of rock it is without parting ways with it?"

"Well, we could cause a small micro fracture in it; just enough to give us some fragments to work with; you know, enough to analyze and catalogue."

"And just how would we do that," Pilates asked?

"There's special equipment at our facility that I can utilize and get the answers but it would risk exposing all of the information to a third party."

"I don't mind so much about the third party as much as I mind about you trying to do all of that on your job. Let me explain one thing doctor; I stole this rock, which is the very same thing that their company charged me with in the beginning. They said I sabotaged their company; well, now I have sabotaged them if they can't generate their business without this rock. I took their trade secrets as well, so you see; I don't want to add aiding and abetting to your resume. I think I still have some of my prize money left. If I get you the equipment you need, can you isolate and analyze the properties of this thing?"

"I can get you started in the right direction but you may have to go elsewhere when it goes beyond my expertise."

"When exactly will that happen?"

"When you get to the stage of carbon dating, which is the point where you will have to determine its age; you will have to get that information from a geophysicist or an astrophysicist. You may also need a chemist to shed light on it composition also. If it is as valuable as you say it is, I can guarantee you that its properties are going to be extremely difficult to find-not impossible-mind you but difficult."

"All I am asking is for you to get it started and we'll go from there. Make a list of all the equipment that you'll need."

"I've still got some of that equipment left over from our last experiments", the doctor confessed.

"Good. We'll use that too. Let's get started!"

The doctor put in for time off from work. He was intrigued about the whole affair of the artifact. He told Pilates that once he had gotten a fractured piece of the metal, Pilates should find a safe place to keep the original piece. He said that they could always say that they found the artifact somewhere and return it later, after they were done with it. Pilates, however, didn't really want to return it at all. He felt that it was better to destroy the rock than to return it.

The doctor ran tests after tests on the item until he felt satisfied that he had come to the end of his knowledge on the subject. He contacted some special scientists and queried them about the dust particle he had taken from the metal. He told them he was willing to send them samples under their strict oath of confidentially. He said the metal seemed to be prehistoric in nature. After receiving their reply, Dr. Marigold sent off three different samples. Although the quantity of the sample was very minute, there was an ample source of the materials given to fully answer the list of prearranged questions that Dr. Marigold sent along with the fragments of the artifact. One of the three scientists, Dr. Carusio Moitreti, physicist and Director of C.E.R.N.; was the same person that had been so valuable to Dr. Marigold in his previous sampling of Pilates hemoglobin. He was hoping that maybe he could shed some light on the mystery surrounding the stone.

Dr. Marigold cross referenced the replies that he had gotten back from all three sources and found that they all agreed on the age of the stone. They said by filtering the artifact through carbon dating and subjecting it to laser spectral analyses; the age of the stone appeared to be about three thousand years old. Dr. Marigold was not one to let pride stand in his way. He was quick to acknowledge that he had miscalculated its age. He thought the artifact was much older than the actual age that it had been given by the three experts. As for the mixture of its composition, he found nothing out of the ordinary: copper, clay, bronze, brass and iron. He saw no mystery there. It appeared to be just a very old piece of metal. Confused and puzzled, Dr. Marigold dropped the glasses that rested on the top of his head onto his nose for one final peek at the specimen under the microscope. He didn't strain to see it nor did he know to especially look for it; but it jumped out at him from the slide of the microscope like it was bigger than a mountain. It was the same antigen, the same mystery X, that he had extrapolated from the blood sample that was taken from Pilates. He wondered how this could be possible. It made Pilates look like some alien life form with three thousand years' worth of DNA encoded in his genes. Who was Pilates exactly?

After careful thought and analyses, the doctor measured his words exactly as to what he was prepared to say to Pilates. He would be brief and to the point. He wanted only to ask him why? Dr. Marigold met Pilates at his home. Pilates seemed eager to finally find out what all the mysterious fuss was about. He was about to find out; but maybe it wasn't the answer that he was expecting.

"Hello doctor. What is the big mystery?"

"Pilates . . ."

"Yes, yes, tell me doc. I've been on pins and needles waiting on you."

"Who are you?"

"What?"

"What are you?"

"What?"

"Why did you do it Pilates?"

"Doctor Marigold, you were supposed to report your findings back to me. Snap out of it. What has happened to you? What kind of questions are those?"

"You lied to us! You set us up so that you could win your award; and then you played us by stealing that little stone to cover everything up. Oh, you had me believing in you. I believed every word you said to me. To think of all the man hours I put into your project, only to find out, it's all a lie. Where are you really from?"

"Doctor, what is wrong with you?"

"It's no use trying to play innocent anymore. The theft of that stone gave you away. Why anybody who had been charged with a crime, would go out and commit the very same crime that they were charged with is beyond irrational. It's downright alien!"

"If you think about it Dr. Marigold, you would see the logic in it. If we are ever confronted with the accusation that we did indeed take the artifact; we would then use the argument that you are presenting to me now; that no one in their right mind would commit the same crime that they had already been charged with and served time for."

"So you admit it?"

"Admit what?"

"Admit it! You are an alien entity!"

"If I didn't know you better doc, I'd say you were crazy. What is all of this about, anyway?"

"I tested the stone. I had it cross-referenced and analyzed, dissected and catalogued. It's just a very old rock, that's it. There is nothing supernatural about it at all; except . . ."

"Except what?"

"Except, I found something that I found before in a place where it should not have been. Traces of your blood are also in that stone. That means that certain cells in your blood are almost three thousand years old!"

"And I am still alive, able to hear you tell me that cockamamie story. How is that possible and why wouldn't I know it if I am an alien?"

"Quit it! It's not working any more. Just tell me the truth and maybe I can help you."

"The truth is, I was just an IT specialist until I met you. I went about . . ."

"What?"

"When I came to you, I was injured with a lacerated arm. It was so badly cut that it needed-I forgot how many stitches . . ."

"Two hundred."

"Look at it! Where is the scar?"

"Yes it's amazing but that what I'm saying, you're not human."

"But you told me at that time, that some foreign body had entered into the wound, creating some mysterious antigen in my blood at the time."

I may have said that but you didn't mention any large artifact like this stone cutting you. You said you were working on a computer. So . . ."

"So that's the answer! That computer must have had some remnant of that stone or some composition of its metallic structure for it to alter my cells like it did. I can remember now; it was a very odd day for me."

"Do you remember where it all happened?" "I know exactly where it happened!"

"If it is like you say then I'll apologize but if not; we'll get you for all of this."

"We've worked too hard and come too far for a silly explanation like aliens to trump the truth. Don't you agree?"

"Yes."

Pilates and Dr. Marigold drove past the large house where Pilates once entered to repair a large computer. "That's it. That's where I almost cut my arm off!"

"Yes, the wound was so evenly cut, our laser couldn't cut it any cleaner. It was a perfect cut. Did you see any kind of metal inside the machine that resembled the stone?"

"No but it got a little hazy once I opened the computer."

"What do you mean?"

"I mean all I can really remember is, going inside that house, looking at a big computer and subsequently getting injured. I remember getting paid though."

"I'm sure of that."

"This isn't a joking matter!"

"I know but the money does always seem to come up in these situations. What else can you recall?"

"His name was Robert Archer. It's all coming back to me now doctor. He was a very strange man. He was elderly but he didn't seem old. He talked about his computer as if it were alive. I remember he had a voice mechanism built into his computer so it could speak to him. The funny thing about it is; I can't remember if it spoke first without any prompting from him or not. Most AI models need some kind of clueing . . ."

"What?"

"He said, decipher its codes. Why would you want an IT specialist to decipher codes; that's a job for a web developer?"

"You mean you don't use codes in your diagnostics?"

"Yes, but he was talking about a larger picture. There was nothing wrong with his computer!"

"But you got paid."

"Doctor not now!"

"No, I'm not joking. I mean, he paid you and you said there wasn't anything wrong with his computer, just now."

"There wasn't, and I told him so but he paid me three hundred dollars anyway."

"He must be wealthy to tip you three hundred dollars just for coming out."

"I ran a diagnostic but I told him there was no charge because I could not find anything wrong."

"Do you give all your clients that kind of break?"

"I was hurt by then and I really needed to get to the hospital."

"I see, and he paid you."

"As a matter of fact, he just about made me take it. He shoved the money into my hand and I took it and left."

"Seems he didn't want you to think too long about him."

"What do you mean doctor?"

"Once a person gets paid, they subconsciously conclude the matter in their mind to be closed. You may think about this and think about that but it always concludes with the idea of payment. Had you not gotten paid, there would have always been a lingering thought in the back of your mind wondering about why you weren't paid."

"That's very, very deep. I never would have thought about that; but you may be right. I always thought about my getting paid when I thought about Mr. Archer. What do you think about the whole situation doc? I mean, you were there from day one. That's when it all began, when I cut my arm."

"Rationally speaking, I see no connections whatsoever," the doctor stated.

"And irrationally," asked Pilates.

"Well, that's a whole different matter. I believe there is a connection with Archer and Regional Slate Institute but I don't know just what that connection is. You are the center piece between them somehow. You are directly connected to each one of them. Thornton and Archer must have some very big secrets. It's just so unconnected that it all seems to add up."

"How," Pilates queried?

"We tried the scientific approach. It gave us some insights to build on. Let's try another angle."

"Like what," Pilates continued?

"First, by getting off of the street that Archer lives on for one thing. We don't want to give him any idea that we're suspicious of him whatsoever. We need to take that stone to an archaeologist; I think we'll have better luck going that route. Since we know the age of it and the composition of it; we can bypass all of that preliminary stuff and get a faster explanation."

"I wish I had your brains doc," Pilates said.

"I wished I had your award," the doctor replied.

Dr. Marigold and Pilates found a very reputable archaeologist that lived in their city. They told him they wanted an assay of the metal alloy artifact that they were about to show him. They wanted to know what it would have been used for in the past and; they also wanted to know if it were a tool, weapon or farmer's implement? Was it from the prehistoric ages, the Bronze Age or the Iron Age? What was the ethnicity of the group that it may have been forged by? They knew it was a lot to ask, for an item so small, but they were now prepared to go all out with the process of discovery to get some answers.

The archaeologist eyed the gray matte triangular shaped artifact. He immediately said, "This relic is one half the size of its original structure."

"Why do you say that," asked Pilates?

"Because," the archaeologist explained, "look at this." He drew a small triangle on a sheet of paper and tore half of it off. He then proceeded to draw another small triangle and likewise tore off half of the other piece of paper. He slid the two pieces of paper together so that they formed a full triangle. They looked at the relic and saw that it really was a portion of a larger triangle. "By the shape and size of this artifact, I would venture to say that it was created to be a weapon. It might have been the tip of a rudimentary spear or the pointed tip of a projectile, maybe an ancient arrow's tip. In any case, this was merely a small remnant of some warrior or hunter's weapon. Tips like these can be found all over Europe on ancient battlefields or from hunting grounds. If you know the age and composition of it like you say, then

I can just about pinpoint the location and the people who may have been the makers of it."

Dr. Marigold and Pilates gave the archaeologist all of the information that they had received on the relic. Upon hearing the information, he immediately started to quote dates and times and names and periods until Pilates slowed him down. "Mr. Fossor, Pilates began, we can't keep up with you."

"It's Fossour," he corrected.

"I am sorry. Mr. Fossour. What exactly was it, a spear or an arrow," Pilates asked?

"It's more of a *gimlet* than anything else."

"A what," asked the doctor?

"A gimlet; a tool used to bore holes into something, a burrower if you will."

"Oh you mean like a drill," Pilates stated.

"Yes, exactly. The person who used the implement was searching for something or expanding his situation."

"By expanding you mean . . ." asked the doctor?

"I mean he could have been boring the soil for food, like for cultivation of the soil. With a dull finish like the relic has though, it's safe to say he wanted the tip to be more aerodynamic than agronomical. That eliminates the farming tool implementation portion of it. That leaves the warrior or hunter option. Since this tip is manufactured with such a keen point, we can assume that it was created to travel a very large distance in a very brief amount of time. A hunter needed that kind of weapon more so than a warrior because in that time period, archers designed their bows so that their arrows used the gravitational pull of the earth to propel them forward to a greater degree in distance. You know, shoot high and let the arc and gravity direct the arrow towards their enemies. However, the hunter had a very short time frame to target his prey and strike with precision. You add this little tip to a very large arrow and you would be very surprised at how far the arrow would go without wind shear and velocity affecting its aim."

"But you said it may have been attached to a spear," Pilates added.

"Yes. That's the problem with *guessimations*. The only thing that would rule out the spear in this case is the total size of the tip. If you're talking about a small rudimentary spear for fishing; this is your tip but if you're talking about a large spear for warfare, then not so much so. So we narrowed it down to spear or arrow. There's one more key element to consider."

"And what's that," the doctor questioned?

"Alchemy."

"What?"

"What!"

"Wait! Before you both get upset, let me explain. It wasn't called alchemy that far back in history, but there was something that was a precursor to alchemy."

"The dark arts," the doctor blandly said.

"Yes."

"How did you two get to that point," asked Pilates?

"There's something strange about the elements that constitutes this composition that you gave me. It is virtually impossible for all of these elements to be present at the same time in this one artifact. This stone represents multiple time periods and yet, it all seems to belong to one particular era. It seems as if the past, present and future combined, merged and became one single point in time-a universal common period in history."

"What," Pilates shouted?

"That's preposterous! That would mean some type of sorcery conjured up the basest element of metals into one huge cauldron and forged a perfect alloy similar to that of steel; and tinged it with an inner layer of gold, "the doctor incredulously cried!

"But where did the gold come from? You didn't mention any gold in the cataloguing," Pilates told the doctor.

"There *was* no listing of gold in the analyses that we got back. I inferred that conclusion when Mr. Fossour told us that he was seriously considering the alchemist influence in the equation," the doctor explained.

"That's correct doctor. Even without the gold being listed, it seems very odd that all of these other metals would be present in this manner here without gold being among them. This metal tip is very rare and it was created with no expenses spared toward its final end. The labor must have been immense. I cannot fathom why so much time and energy would be placed into a single artifact of this size and proportion unless it was created to be a rulers' scepter or a symbol to represent his power."

"And you were saying that the place of its origin would be . . .," asked the doctor anxiously?

"Shinar."

"Where?"

"Babylon."

"How do you know . . .?"

"The flint mixture of the tip leads one to the conclusion that this particular item was meant to have a one way journey; it wasn't ever going to be reused. It was set ablaze with molten fire and shot aloft at a high piercing speed. Its purpose was to bore a pathway though the heavens to wound its intended prey."

"And you can ascertain all of that from this small piece of metal," asked Pilates.

"Yes, from your sample and from our history. The questions lead me to the answer. After you told me the chronological age of this relic, I deduced the obvious. This is a product of the Stone Age as you can see by the small embedded ancient stones. Yet, it has the Bronze Age, the Copper Age and Iron Age all visible in its composite makeup. Unless we have a time traveler from each of those periods working in unison with other people from different eras who had a common purpose in mind; then we must conclude that some dark spiritual forces must have united and descended upon humankind at a single point in time and led to the development of this weapon."

"Is it worth anything," Pilates asked?

"That's according to whom you would ask. I would say, coupled with its age and history; this tip could fetch a very handsome price, a very handsome price indeed. But from the historical viewpoint, I would think it belongs in a museum, because if you still had practitioners of the now defunct dark arts out there; and somehow this artifact fell into their hands; this item could be a very dangerous tool."

Pilates quickly paid Fossour and motioned for the doctor to follow him. He didn't want to give out any more information than he had to, and risk Fossour piecing events together until he became fully aware of all that they knew. Pilates didn't know what they were going to do with the information that they had just acquired but he knew they couldn't get Fossour involved any deeper.

"Thank you Mr. Fossour. You've been invaluable," the doctor remarked.

"We can't thank you enough," Pilates added.

"Why are we rushing Pilates?"

"I didn't want to divulge any more information. Mr. Fossour was putting all of the data that we gave him into a perfect piece. He would have begun to ask us questions. I wasn't ready for that; were you?"

"No but, I had a few more questions that I wanted to ask him. He was very knowledgeable."

"That's exactly why we shouldn't stay any longer. Thank goodness for all of that useful information he gave us. The only thing I cannot figure out is; how did Thornton and his men get this thing to work for them? All in all, it's still just an inanimate object. We've had it in our possession for a while now and it hasn't given us any reason to believe that it has influenced us with any kind of mysterious persuasion as it did to Thornton and his group."

"I don't know Pilates. We could very well be under this things' spell right now and not even know it."

"We'll take it back to the group and let them decide whether or not it has some hidden agenda attached to it."

"Sounds good to me. You know I'm a practical individual, and for me, to see myself talking about rocks and stones and metal having influence on people; well, it just goes against the grain for me."

"You didn't see how they were talking about this thing at their headquarters doctor. It sounded just like the same way that Archer fellow talked about his computer. I heard them conversing in a way that was just plain peculiar. We need another look at Archers' computer. All of this is going to take some time-time that we don't have. The coordinating committees of the international community are going to be screaming bloody murder if we don't resolve this thing very soon. They're waiting for us doc. They're going to be growing impatient in a little while. I hope they saw a glimpse of the event that I was talking about, twenty four hours after the awards presentation, just like I promised them."

"I'm sure they did Pilates. We would have heard something from them by now if they hadn't experienced something."

"Doctor, call John and ask him to get in contact with some of the international members. Tell him to check in on them so we can be sure we're still in the clear with them."

"Alright. 'Hello John, Pilates wants you to contact some of the members of the international project team. He wants you to find out if everything is going alright with them. And . . . oh, that's great news. I'll be sure and tell him. Congratulations to you both."

"What's that all about doctor?"

"John and Peggy Lee are engaged to be married."

"What? When was he going to tell me?"

"He said he was going to surprise you; but that you were out running so many errands until he figured he'd better not wait too long. He says they haven't set the date yet but it's going to be fairly soon."

"Good for him. I was always a little concern about John. We're not getting any younger you know; I'm twenty six and John is sixty two years old. That's old enough to be my father and he still thinks he works for me. I told him countless times that we're partners but he always reverts back to our old business venture days. Much as I hate to say it doc, I sort of miss those days now. I felt freer then than I do now. I knew my purpose and I enjoyed what I did for a living."

"And now?"

"Now I have some worldwide view of a bonded humanity, united in a common cause to become one once again with a universal speech. What about that doctor?"

"Don't ask me, I'm only here for your blood!"

Pilates laughed along with the doctor for a while; temporarily relieving the enormous burden that one would associate with a plan that encompassed dealing with an entire population of all the people of the earth.

"Good morning. We are here to see the assistant director."

"Good morning sirs. Mr. Chambers, there are two gentlemen here to see you."

"What are your names please?"

"I am Inspector Raymond Simmons and this is Inspector Paul Dunavant. We are from the firm of Dunavant and Simmons Private Investigations. We have an appointment with Mr. Chambers."

"Mr. Chambers sir; they are from the investigation firm of Dunavant and Simmons. Yes sir. Please follow Bob. He'll show you where you need to go."

"This way gentleman, follow me."

"Here you are, Mr. Chambers office."

"Good morning gentlemen, may I offer you a cup of coffee, espresso or refreshments?"

"No thank you."

"No thank you."

"Well as I stated to you earlier, this case should have the highest classification of confidentiality.

Mr. Richard Thornton, our director, has gone missing. He was last seen leaving the court house where he had testified earlier in a case concerning industrial espionage and sabotage."

"I am Raymond Simmons; I shall ask you a few pertinent questions; and that is Mr. Paul Dunavant; he will only take notes and summarize the information that you give to us, but none of the information that you give to us, shall ever leave this room. Before we begin . . . Paul you may get started."

"What is he doing?"

"He is just completing a clean sweep of your office to make sure that you're not bugged or surveilled in any kind of way."

"Do you think that's necessary?"

"If it's a matter of industrial espionage or sabotage as you say; the perpetrators would definitely go to great lengths to insure that they know your every move. Was the guy that Mr. Thornton testified against convicted?"

"Yes he was, but he didn't receive as much time as we would have liked for him to receive."

"Is he still serving his sentence?"

"As far as we know. He was sentenced to two years-one year of probation and one year to be served with the possibility of parole in six months."

"That's more of a slap on the wrist, wouldn't you say?"

"Well, we underestimated his lawyer, I guess. We had everything under control until Richard went missing. I heard he took ill on the stand and just disappeared without a trace. The jury found the guy guilty on just one count. Richard assured us that he was going to be sentenced to twenty years in prison. We just didn't know what to do after we lost Richard. And there's another issue involved in this case; a missing item we would like for you to investigate its whereabouts, which is just as important to us as finding Richard."

"What is it?"

"The guy they sent away to prison may have had an accomplice because we have had a break-in while he is in prison. They took a very valuable icon from our vault. It is so valuable that we cannot continue to carry on our day to day business operation without it. You can tell by the size of your contracts, how much we want this item back. We have stipulated in your contract this specific clause which I now reiterate to you; the faster you find the item we seek, the more incentives we will pay you. For every day under the day that you have agreed upon with us, the item is returned; we shall pay an additional one hundred thousand dollars apiece to you. Do you think that is a fair offer?"

"Very fair. Wouldn't you say Mr. Dunavant?"

"I agree. It's more than fair."

"So you say that in two weeks' time, we should have our property back, safe and sound."

"I didn't quite say that we can guarantee the condition of the object upon retrieval. We don't quite know the mindset of the individual who stole your property. If he stole the item for revenge, he may very well destroy it before we can ascertain who he is." "Gentlemen, gentlemen, that's not acceptable. I heard that you two were the best investigators in America. I have told you how important this *precious stone* is to us. You must give me your solemn oath to find it and to find it quickly."

"Mr. Dunavant and I are the best at what we do. We shall find this item for you! However, even though we are the best investigators that you can find; we cannot guarantee that whoever took your item has not destroyed it already. We can guarantee that we shall find the person who stole it."

"Alright! Alright. Just make a mental note that we could care less about the person who stole our property. We don't want justice. We just want our property back. If you find the individual and he seems reasonable, we are prepared to pay whatever he asks."

Paul Dunavant took off his black fedora and scratched his head.

"I was thinking the same thing Paul. What kind of property are we talking about here, Mr. Chambers."

"That's part of our contract, remember? There is to be no questions concerning the item in question. It is simply for trade secrets provisions that we aren't allowed to discuss it. Understand?"

"We got you. We'll get it back for you in one week!"

"Very good."

The pair of investigators, famous for their quick successive case endings, went straight to Sidney Green Minimum Correctional facility. They proceeded to quickly eliminate any trails that was of no consequence in their investigation of the missing artifact or of the missing Richard Thornton. They now realized that the recovery of the missing artifact took precedent over the disappearance of Richard Thornton.

"Mr. Mulberry, we are here to inquire about one of your inmates; Pilates Daniels is his name. We would like to speak to him if we could, please."

"And who might you be?"

"We are private investigators trying to solve a particular case where your inmate might have some relevant information that may help us with our investigation. We would greatly appreciate it if we could just talk to him for a couple of minutes."

"Sure thing, have a seat; I'll have the guard bring him up in just a minute. He's one of our celebrity inmates you know. Did you know he won a Nobel Prize in science? He doesn't have to be here with us very much longer though. He'll be getting out on parole in a couple of months. Oh, Darren, go and bring Daniels up front. These gentlemen have a few questions for him."

"Are you Pilates Daniels?"

"Yes."

"We just want to ask you a few questions. This has nothing to do with your time spent here. Your answers shall be kept in the strictest confidential regards. We understand that you are serving time here for stealing trades secrets from Regional Slate Language Institute Corporation. We wanted to know who hired you and what did you do with those trade secrets?"

"I told them at the trial that I was innocence. They didn't believe me so here I am. It's no big deal though; I'm just about to be release in a couple of months anyway."

"Yeah but the evidence was a bit overwhelming that pointed to you. It's a miracle that you got off with such a light sentence. Do you have any strong feeling towards the Institute for being responsible for putting you here?"

"Like I said, that's almost all behind me now. I don't think I'm going to give them a second thought once I get out of here. I think I have other things to do once I get out."

"Here's our card. My name is Raymond Simmons and that is Paul Dunavant. If you think of anything that you may have forgotten since you were first incarcerated, don't hesitate to call us. We may have a reward for you if you have the right information that we're looking for. We may even be able to help you find the person that you believe framed you. Don't forget: Dunavant and Simmons."

"OK."

The team of Dunavant and Simmons proceeded to the court house where they found two bailiffs who were working the trials on the particular day that the inspectors were now investigating. They asked the two bailiffs to answer a few questions about the day in which Richard Thornton disappeared.

The first bailiff, whose name was Charlie Woodson, answered inspector Simmons first question," I was standing at the door that day when I saw Mr. Richard Thornton get up from the witness box and slowly walked down the aisle towards me. He seemed to be dazed. I heard his attorney explain to the judge that his client wasn't feeling very well that day so I dismissed the thought of how odd he looked, because he did look sick to me."

"Did you notice the direction he was going in?"

"I followed him until he got to the top of the court house stairs. As he began a slow descent down the stairs, I turned and was heading back into the court room; when I gradually looked back, I saw him and then he was gone. I mean when I saw him, he was midways down the stairs and about two seconds later; he had vanished. Who can descend that many steps in two seconds? He must have flown down them. I remember thinking that compared to the slow walk he had before; he must not have felt as bad as we all thought."

"And You? What's your name?"

"My name is Tom Henderson. I saw just about the same thing that Charlie saw except the part where he says Thornton went down the stairs."

"What do you mean?"

"I was stationed outside the court room when Thornton came out. He didn't head for the stairs when I saw him. That's why I got a little confused when I saw Charlie come outside the court room as if he was following someone as he would normally do when they would leave the court room. Charlie walked to the edge of the stairs and he looked as if he was watching somebody, but then I saw him shake his head and turn around to go back inside the court house."

"Where did you see Thornton go?"

"He came out and he turned right. Then I took my focus off of him for a moment when I saw Charlie come out. I never looked Thornton's way again. I'm sorry; I didn't know he was going to go missing. I'm sorry."

"Take it easy. We're not here to point fingers and cast blame on anyone. We're here to find two things. Those two things are beginning to look more and more intertwined than ever. When we find one, we will most assuredly find the other. Don't you agree Mr. Dunavant? I thought so."

They gave the two bailiffs their cards and asked them to call if they thought of any other pertinent information concerning Richard Thornton. They decided to pay Pilates' project group a little visit next. The inspectors had a very successful strict formula that they adhered to almost to the letter. They had been successful in their career ninety-nine percent of the time but they only concerned themselves mostly with the failure of that one percent.

John was amazed when he saw the two inspectors arrive at the door of the project complex seeking answers. He grew extremely nervous. He thought they may have been highly paid bounty hunters. He spoke as little as possible so that he wouldn't accidentally give a hint of information concerning Pilates.

"Good day sir. Can we ask you a few questions?"

"What is this concerning?"

"There's nothing to be alarmed about. We are hired investigators contracted to find Mr. Richard Thornton who has been missing now for quite some time. Now we know about your dealings with his company. We assure you that our presence here has nothing to do with the events that transpired between his company and your enterprise."

John became even more confused. He felt as if he was having a panic attack of some kind. "John, when you talk to Pi, tell him . . ."

"Peggy, these gentlemen are hired inspectors that have come here trying to get some information about Richard Thornton whereabouts. Gentlemen, this is my fiancée Peggy Lee."

"How do you do?"

"Nice to meet you ma'am."

"Anyway gentlemen, we don't have dealings with that company so we don't know anything about Thornton's disappearance."

"We're just canvassing all the leads possible. We're not here in any disparaging way to say that someone connected to your project is responsible for his disappearance. We just have to check all of our leads; understand? Good. Have a nice day."

"Hello John. Yes, he's with me right now. What? Yes, I'll tell him. That's right. Uh huh. Yes. Are you alright John? You sound stressed. OK. Just relax and take a couple of deep breaths. Everything is going to be alright. We'll be in shortly. See you later."

"What's wrong?"

"Something appears to be very wrong back at the complex. I think John had an anxiety attack or panic attack or something. He was trying to tell me what happened but he was mixing his angst between each and every word that he was saying, until I just had to stop him and I told him to calm down."

"But what was it that he was so alarmed about?"

"He said two inspectors came around looking for answers to Richard Thornton disappearance."

"What?! I would have had an anxiety attack too if I were there. Why would they go there anyway? That doesn't make sense. Regional Slate must have hired them to find the artifact and they're using Thornton as a smoke screen to do it. They suspect that I broke in and took it and they're right this time."

"Hold on Pilates, we don't know that. It could have been just like John said. Thornton *has* been missing for a while now, you know."

"Yeah, I can still see his . . ."

"What's wrong?"

"Thornton's face was looking just like the inmates faces that day."

"Don't start Pilates. We need to let that night go."

"I know, but it just occurred to me that the look on his face at the trial when he got up out of the witness box and was walking out the door completely oblivious to his surroundings; that look was identical to the inmates' faces, which I got a chance to see up close and personal. There is something that is going on here that's not quite right doctor."

"I know of a lot of things going on that's not quite right. It's been that way ever since I met you!"

"Seriously, I'm starting to have second thoughts about the project."

"I don't believe what I'm hearing. To you, the project is everything."

"It's funny that you should say that. I remember hearing almost exactly the same words coming from Archer. He said that his machine was his everything. I cringed when he said it and I should be cringing now while you're saying it."

"But you're not."

"No I'm not. What's happening to me doc?"

"All jokes aside, that's why I'm here. I'm going to keep an eye on your condition. I'll tell you one thing I have observed; while I'm in your presence, the world sure takes on a different appearance. When you're away, it goes back to normal. Maybe I'm getting caught up in all the hysteria surrounding your meteoric rise to fame."

"You told me a lot just now doctor. It's not just my project that's causing the problem. It's the foreign bodies in my blood; it's the artifact that I took from their company; it's Thornton, Archer and Regional Corporation. As much as I hate to say this, I feel that I should cancel the project and concentrate on finding out how much damage has already been done."

"You know, I don't really have a say one way or the other concerning the matter, but haven't you put a lot of time and effort in this project? How are the other people in your group going to respond to this; those people who have labored so diligently to make your quest a success? You've received over a million dollars in prize money that was dependent on the promise you made that you would see this thing through."

"I'll tell them I'll pay it back. I'll give my medal back too. We must get to the bottom of this thing once and for all before it gets out of hand."

"Do what you think is best."

"We need to see Archers' machine. After we go in and talk with the group about everything we've discussed; we need to devise a way for us to get into Archer's house without raising his suspicions and see for ourselves what the great mystery is all about? This time I can be objective because you're going with me."

"I hope I can be of help."

"I just want to say that it has been great working with all of you guys . . ."

"Hey Pi, what's going on? What happened?"

"It's hard for me to say this after we've come so far but for my own conscience's sake, I feel have to say it."

"Say what? Tell us Pi. What's wrong?"

"I may have been wrong with the conclusions that I came up with at the beginning with my proposals to the project."

"How?"

"Yes, how?"

"As you all know, when our project got under way, I told you that there was going to be a singular event that was going to change everything and everyone all at once in the world. I thought that it was something that the Regional Corporation was doing, in an effort to try and stop us from succeeding; but now it appears something is happening to them too. I feel our project may be causing irreparable damage to our world. We must shut it down before it's too late."

"What are you talking about Pi? We don't see any damage or any problems."

"I know but they're here all the same even if you can't see it. We are going, the doc and I, and maybe John; we are going to try and get to the bottom of this. We need to know if we are doing any harm and causing damage and bringing suffering to people's lives. If we are, then we need to stop it now before it's too late."

"What are you going to do?"

"It's just like the last time. The less you know, the better it is for you. There are now investigators coming around. It's strange that they're asking for Thornton instead of inquiring about my whereabouts or the whereabouts of the Institutes' property. It's so confusing until it makes sense. Our project has something to do with this. After we get information from the Archer's residence, we shall move forward from there. All those who don't wish to help at this time should go, so they aren't involved any further. We understand and support you. Please don't feel you're letting me down by leaving. I appreciate each and every one of you regardless if you go or stay."

"We ain't going nowhere!"

"Thanks Stanley! John, I need you to dig up the old file on Archer. Set up a free in home consultation. Tell him we are going to do a follow up on all of our client's work."

"What if he recognizes you Pi? You are a celebrity now, you know."

"Funny, I don't feel like one John. Anyway, doc, here, is going to be my boss. He is going to keep Mr. Archer occupied while I search for our missing link in his machine. If I find it, I'm going to rip it out and replace it with another part so he won't know what hit him. It shouldn't take me long to get it. The main thing is to keep him talking about other things. Don't let him bring the conversation back to his computer or we'll be in trouble. Who knows what kind of safeguards he has in place. After the little chat that we had with Mr. Fossour, I'm very nervous considering the potential power Archer must possess."

"Don't worry Pi; I'll be in the van . . ."

"I don't want you out there on this one John. You stay here with Peggy Lee and wait for doc's call. If something goes wrong, you can call the police. That's right! Call the police. At least I'll be in a safe prison rather than who knows where with that guy. Everybody's on the same page?"

"What if he asks me something particular about his computer?"

"Listen doc, you're a doctor; talk to him until he's blue in the face. Any topic, any subject; go to another room, just keep his mind occupied."

"OK."

"Hello, may I speak to Robert Archer. Mr. Archer, this is Daniels Den Computer repair. We've done some work on your computer a while back and we're updating all of our customer's computers free of charge. Yes, but our updates are a lot different than those you get online. Our updates actually update old parts and refurbish your memory so that it lasts longer and functions faster than if it were the newest computer out on the market. We pride ourselves in treating your computer just like it's part of your *family*. Great! When is a good time for you? Tomorrow? Excellent. Do you still reside at the same location? You do? You should see him arrive there first thing in the morning. Our repair truck is in the shop so he'll be in a van on this trip. Thank you for your business and we're pleased to service your computer again."

"Are you ready doc? We can do this. Take your time. When you see me give you the signal, let's get the hell out of there, alright?"

"OK."

"Let's go!"

"Good morning, it's so nice to see you again. Come on in. Excuse me. Who is this?"

"This is my boss. You can call him Tom. He comes out on the follow ups to make sure the customers are fully satisfied."

"I was under the impression that you owned your business."

"That's the thing about work, Mr. Archer, everybody got a boss."

"What a nice home you have Mr. Archer. You wouldn't mind if I just peeked at a couple of rooms would you? Maybe a small tour. I was thinking along these lines if ever I got myself into a position where I can afford something like this. What line of work are you in?"

"I was in exploration for a great deal of my career."

"That's sort of an old time profession, isn't it? I mean we have space exploration and deep sea exploration but just exploration. Most of our land mass has been charted, hasn't it?"

"Well, you see, I was a big game hunter in Africa at one time. I explored the dark continent for pleasure and for my business. When governments started to outlaw hunting because of endangered species and animal rights I slowly became extinct myself."

"I never heard of retirement put exactly that way but it does have a certain poetic ring to it."

"Oh no! I may be getting on in years but I am not retired yet."

"Maybe I missed what you said but I could have sworn you were talking about retirement."

"I can't hunt anymore but that doesn't mean that I am not a hunter anymore. Why, Bo . . . let's go and see how my updates are coming along." "Oh, you don't have to worry about that. Our technician always alerts when his work is done. I just find it's fascinating in this day and age that I can actually say I met a big game hunter. Where is your trophy room?"

"As I said, there's a growing distaste in the present culture of today concerning stuffed animal trophies, even if the animal is a predator. I understand that and therefore I relinquished all of my trophies but one."

"Which trophy did you keep?"

"I kept Bo!"

"Bo?"

"Yes! My bowman series 9000. Don't you remember? You barely noticed my bo when you came in. You complimented me on my home but you made no mention whatsoever about bo. Who are you?"

"I just wanted to give my tech room to work plus I was fascinated by your profession. I still would like to hear more about your time in Africa."

"Maybe another time. You've seen just about all of my home so I think we can get back so I can find out how my updates are coming along doctor."

"OK . . . hey what did you call me? My name is Tom!"

"You just remind me of a doctor that's all. I apologize. Shall we go now?"

"Oh. Yes I suppose so."

"And how are we doing, Mr. Daniels?"

"What?"

"How are we doing?"

"I'm done."

"You know Mr. Daniels; I was somewhat perplexed by the fact that you still repair computers even though you won a Nobel Prize. You even have a boss man overseeing your work. It seems to me you should have a staff working for you. But the strangest thing is; you didn't win your award in technology, now did you? You won your award in a field that bo knows all too well. Bo, what has he been doing to you?"

'He's been searching to see if I have the SLATE inside of my circuitry Robert. He has been relentlessly searching for it. Shall I tell him Robert? Shall I enlighten him now?'

"Feel free bo. Tell him."

'The SLATE is not in my circuitry boards. *I am* the SLATE!'

"What is it talking about? I have been looking for damaged and overheated circuitry components inside of this computer. I find it most fascinating that it can actually converse with you. However, by the erroneous assumption that it concluded about the work that I was doing on it; I must conclude that its' programming must be systemically flawed. How else can a machine be so bold as to actually try to judge factually any of my motives towards its repair? What is the SLATE?"

"Although you feign ignorance to everything Mr. Daniels; your peculiar pronunciation of the SLATE leads me to believe otherwise. One cannot pronounce the SLATE like you have unless they have been in direct contact with it."

"If what you say is true, then why have you kept up with this charade? Why did you allow us to come back and diagnosed your computer again? Why didn't you just call the police? What is the SLATE?"

"Bo, I don't think our friends here quite understand it all yet."

"Hey! What's happening? How did all of the windows and doors automatically shut like that?"

"Doctor, don't concern yourself at all with that. Concern yourself with this!"

"Doc!!"

"He'll be alright, in the next life!"

"What have you done? You've killed him!"

"I didn't do a thing. Bo, what have you done?"

'I shot an arrow in the air,
Where it landed I know not where!'

"That was naughty Bo-very naughty!"

"What do you want with me?"

"Who said I wanted anything to do with you? You came here under false pretenses. You tried to destroy Bo. You had everything at your disposal. You had the world: money, fame and power. What did you do with it but come back here to ask me some asinine questions about some word that you already know the meaning of? You are free to go any time you feel like it. Bo won't stop you and I definitely won't do anything to keep you here any longer. Go! Don't ever come back!"

"What about the doctor?"

"Can he heal himself?"

"Pilates, what's the matter? You look like you've seen a ghost? Where's the doctor? What happened Pi?"

"The doctor's dead! Archer killed him!"

"What? What do mean? Why didn't you call me like you said you would? Did you leave the doc behind? Why?"

"I thought he was going to kill me too. He didn't, for some reason or another, but I thought he was. I couldn't help doc. You should have seen how he looked at me right before he . . ."

"Snap out of it Pi! It's not your fault!"

"Like hell it ain't! Doc didn't have to come along with me. I could have tried to do it myself. I should have told him to stay away. I just felt a little safer with the doc with me. I should have told him to stay away!"

"Just like you told me to stay away? Pi, all of this seems to be happening for a reason. Doc knew the risks before he went with you; just like I was ready to take those very same risks myself. The thing you need to do is; get your mind focused on the task at hand. We need to get that madman. For doc's sake, we need to get him."

"Mr. Dunavant, did you see the look on Mr. Palley's face when he opened his door to us? I explained it to him just as plain as I could that we weren't concerned with any of the history that had transpired between their company and the Institute. He couldn't hear it. He looked like he was trying his best to protect someone. When his fiancée entered the room and asked him about our guy, he completely silenced her. He didn't think we would notice that. He didn't know you have an insanely accurate discerning eye. What do you think? Should we follow this trail? I thought so."

"Hello operator, I lost my cell phone and all of my records with it. Yes, I've gotten another phone and I want to keep everything exactly the same. However, can you forward to me some of my prior calls so that I can get some of my old contact numbers to add to my new phone? Password? Wait a second; I seem to have forgotten it. One moment please. Mr. Dunavant, I need their password. What? Really? OK. My password is Pilates Project. Thank you. You're a genius Mr. Dunavant! The records are coming in now. I'll make a copy of them and . . . wait! Why is there a great big asterisk marked beside this name? I see they made a recent call to him also. Robert Archer. Let's pay him a visit Mr. Dunavant and see what he has to do with this small mystery."

"Hello. Who? Oh. I'm his assistant John Palley. Can I take a message? Jim Bainberry from the Nobel Prize committee? Yes I understand. I'll have him give you a call as soon as he gets in. You're welcome.

Pilates, you won't believe who that was. It was Jim Bainberry from the Nobel Prize committee. He says the committee is getting somewhat impatient not hearing from you. They saw a little something happening in the world after you left; and they were thrilled by it, but then it all went away. They're not disappointed. They just want more."

"I already told you John I'm through with that project. I was telling doc about it and he understood. He told me to do what I thought was best. If you and Peggy Lee weren't engaged to be married; I'd say let's go back there to Archer's house and burn it down to the ground."

"What's stopping us?"

"No John. This time, I go alone."

"What about Bainberry?"

"Call him back and tell him that I want to return my prize. I don't know about the prize money yet but, I have to come up with the full amount that they gave me so that I could repay them. That's going to be the hard part; coming up with a million dollars."

"Don't worry about the money right now Pi; they may even offer you some kind of deal; so first things first."

"You're right John. First I need to get Archer!"

Knock. Knock. "Good day gentlemen. May I help you?"

"Yes you may. We work for Regional Slate Language Institute Corporation . . ."

"A very fine organization."

"Yes, uh, anyway can we ask you a few questions?"

"By all means, come on in."

"My name is Raymond Simmons and this gentleman is . . ."

"Yes I know, Mr. Paul Dunavant."

"That is correct sir."

"Mr. Dunavant has some unique talents. Does he not?"

"That is also correct. Where do you get your information sir? You seem to be well informed about things."

"Let's just say that I have a little inside information."

"Well, that's good because we hope your inside information can help lead us to the director of that company."

"And why should I know that?"

"You mean to tell Mr. Dunavant and myself that you have no interest whatsoever in the Institute."

"I did not say that I had no interest in that company. I merely asked, why you think that I would know anything about Thornton's disappearance."

"How did you know his name sir? We didn't tell you his name."

"I read gentlemen. He has been missing for quite some time now. I think his first disappearance was at the trial of that guy who sabotaged their company."

"Did you ever meet him personally?"

"What are you implying?"

"Look! We are behind our time frame here. It usually doesn't take us over a week to solve our cases. The prepaid fee we get for early disposition of our cases are astounding. Now we are almost over our time limit. We are not implying anything. We want to solve this case in two days' time or our money is forfeited! Do you understand? If you know something about Thornton; tell us now, because if we find out that you do know something without telling us; well, you'll get a first-hand look at Mr. Dunavant special talent. Do I make myself clear?"

"Crystal."

'Have you had any contact with Pilates Daniels?"

"Gentlemen, gentlemen, please, we are all on the same team here. I mean, I would love to help you solve your case so that you can receive your untold millions; but the fact of the matter is; for the first time, I'm at a loss here to explain the implications of what all have transpired concerning your precious case. What I will tell you is this; that fellow, Pilates, is at the root of all of this trouble. He may have even hired someone to kidnap Thornton as far as we know. So, you should start and end your courageous investigation with him and not me. Good Day gentlemen."

"Mr. Dunavant, somehow I got the feeling he knew all about us and the case as if he were our employer. How could that be? You think he has some ties to Regional? You do! Well why didn't he just say so and dispense with all the hokey-pokey antics? What? He did? When? When did he tell us that he was paying our salary? I missed that one. He's our boss? Mr. Dunavant, you might have missed this one. You remember when you missed . . . ok. Ok. You haven't been wrong since."

"Gentlemen, I know that we said one week tops. This case seems to be highly unusual though. Mr. Dunavant just intimated to me the other day that it seemed as if some sort of magic was involved. I know how absurd that may sound to you but, believe me when I say; if Mr. Dunavant says that's what it is; then that's what it is."

"Mr. Simmons, you promise that you would have both the SLATE and Richard Thornton back within a week. It's been six days. Unless you, at the very least, discover the whereabouts of the SLATE in one day's time; you'll forfeit all of your incentive bonuses."

"Mr. Chambers, we've covered more ground in six days' time than all other private investigators could have uncovered in a year. Yet, you're acting like we somehow dropped the ball on this. All we're asking for is an extension on our contract for one more week. We came across this individual. He seemed somewhat remotely connected to your corporation. He wouldn't come out and tell us plainly what his connection to your company is for some reason."

"Who is this individual that you're talking about Mr. Simmons?"

"His name is Robert Archer. Mr. Dunavant seems to feel that he is the head of your corporation."

"What? What makes you say that?"

"If Thornton is executive director of your company; then tell me, who is the owner of your business?"

"We don't rightly know. He has remained anonymous to us all these years. We do know that Thornton had an inside path to the owner's council. If this gentleman you are referring to is indeed the owner of the corporation; then he would show it by aggressively seeking to get Thornton back at all cost!"

"According to Mr. Dunavant, that is exactly what he did. He tipped his hand Mr. Chambers without even knowing it. The very best private investigator in the world would not have come away with that information, so you see; you're getting a great return for your money. Give us that extra week and who knows what else we might turn up for you in the process."

"What say ye members of the council? The *ayes have it*! Alright, we'll give you one more week. We agree that you have had quite a bit of success in a very short period of time and if this Mr. Archer is truly our leader, then it would be very well worth every penny that you shall receive."

"Pilates, stop and think of what you're doing. Destroying that computer is one thing but killing Archer is murder! I can't let you do it and ruin your life. I hate that he killed the doctor as much as you do but I know there is a better way to go about it than this."

"What better way is there John? I know you mean well and I appreciate it too, but if you had seen the doctor in the state that he was in; I'm very sure you would be doing exactly what I'm about to do."

"What's your plan Pi? What's after you execute your plan? What then?"

"The plan is to burn Archer's house down to the ground. If I come across him, the plan is to take him out too; that's my plan in its entirety."

"When questions are asked about who started the fire and cries are heard, screaming arson and murder; tell me Pilates, what's your plan after that?"

"I told you before that you're not coming; so stop worrying about all of that, alright? This has got to be done."

"Let the police handle it Pi. Please! If you remember how you felt when the doctor was killed; imagine how I'll feel if something like that were to happen to you."

"What do you suggest then? Should we let him get away with murder? How can the police help? I didn't see Archer actually kill the doctor."

"How did he die then?"

"That damned computer was talking so much gibberish. I hate it!"

"Gibberish? Exactly what did the computer say Pi?"

"Some strange lyric about shooting an arrow in the air. Archer just loves everything that stupid computer says. He became exhilarated at the tone of the machine. All of this was happening while doc was dying."

"It makes no sense Pi. What does shooting an arrow in the air has to do with Archer becoming excited at doc's death?"

"Mr. Fossour, the archeologist, told us something John. He told doc and me that the artifact that we got from the Institute may have belonged to a ruler or a great hunter. Ever since I started my project, I have been thinking about something that has stayed with me from my youth."

"What's that Pi?"

"I first heard about it in church a long time ago. It was the story of Babel."

"Yeah. I was trying to relate that story to you when you first started your project too. But I know now that your project has nothing to do with that story."

"Are you sure John? I mean think about it. Could it all be so huge of a coincidence that it's comical? Nimrod was a great hunter. He was mighty with his Bow and arrow. There was none in all the land more expertly adept with that weapon than he was. And now we have *Archer* and his computer, the *Bowman* 9000. It didn't even cross my mind until that computer said that gibberish phrase. Even after we received all of that information from the archaeologist, it all didn't settle in until that stupid phrase came from that computer. You should have seen the delight on Archer's face as doc took his last breath. I can't get that jingle out of my mind."

"What jingle was it, Pi?"

'I shot an arrow in the air, where it landed I know not where.'

I hate that machine John!"

"I know you do Pi. I'm coming with you and this time you can't stop me."

"May we see Chief Director Carson Mulberry? We've been here before. He knows us. Director Mulberry, can we talk to Pilates? Yes, we have a couple of additional questions for him. Oh yeah, he was more than helpful the last time we saw him. As a matter of fact, he'll probably put the finishing touches on this case today. That's right. That's why it's imperative that we see him. Thank you so much. Hey Pilates. Remember us? We remembered after we left that we had a few more questions that were left unanswered the last time we saw you. Do you remember Mr. Archer?"

"Yes. I serviced his computer once. Why?"

"He thinks you know more than you are letting on to about the case that we are investigating. He thinks you have a larger knowledge on the disappearance of Richard Thornton."

"What's all of this about Thornton? The last time I saw him was in the court room. Why is he missing? I've been here in this facility for all of this time and I assure you that I didn't hire anyone to kidnap or kill Thornton. It doesn't make sense that he should so suddenly disappear."

"Something else disappeared from the Regional Corporation."

"What was it?"

"You mean you don't know?"

"Is this some kind of a trick question? Are you trying to reopen my case so I can get more time for that trumped up charge that they put me in here for in the first place; if so, it's not going to work?"

"Look I'm going to level with you, alright? This is the only time that I'm going to offer this choice to you so pay very close attention. My client, the Institute, doesn't care about what you did before. They don't necessarily appreciate that their director is missing, because that is not their number one priority at this particular time. Their number one priority is getting back their property, plain and simple. It's a very small artifact; however, this artifact is the basis upon which their entire foundation is built upon. They are telling us that if they get the item back, they will give you a reward! Got that? They are actually willing to pay you for your time spent in here and pay you for the recovery of the artifact. Sounds like a super good deal to me. So where is the item?"

"Evidently you guys must have thought that I was lying to you before when I said that I was innocent. I really don't know anything else. You should believe me now because my time here is almost served. I would be the first person to tell everything if I had a story to tell."

"Remember, we won't be as pleasant the next time that you see us if you are lying to us. As a matter of fact you might want to change your name and skip the country if we have to come back here again. You have closed the door on your final opportunity!"

"What?"

"Hello mom. I miss you and dad. I want to get out of here now. I know I don't have but a little over a month to go. Something just doesn't seem right in here. I wish I knew what it was. Misha? When? She hasn't come to see me yet. On Monday? Thanks mom. I'll be glad to see her. Bye."

"John, maybe you're right. I thought about it and reason came out on top."

"You're not changing your mind just because I said I was coming along with you, are you Pi?"

"No, I need to look at the larger picture just like you said. I need to implement the full shut down of Pilate's project. I need to end the signal synchronization from all of our satellites and I need to restore the right order in the world. That should be my main goal now."

"What will the side effects be Pi? What will happen to us? There are so many people who have taken your shots that it would be a catastrophe if there are any major side effects at all when your project cease to be in existence. I think the majority of people thought your project would last indefinitely. Shouldn't you do a test run first to find out about any unexpected mishaps that might occur?"

"As always John, you make a good point, but I need to hurry and contact NASA to see if they can cancel the signals before it's too late. Do you think that you can get through to the right people there so we can cut through the red tape? If not, I'll have to go to Florida to personally get it done myself."

"I'll call them right now Pi and find out."

"Hello NASA, this is John Palley with the Pilates project. I am assistant project manager. What is the protocol for ending the satellites' directional signals synchronization with each other? Yes sir, we want to pull the plug on it. You need Pilates' authorization? He can fax his authorization to you or he can send it by e-mail. No. No telephone calls. I have full authorization to make this decision. Look at our contract that we have with you. That's right. Give our international neighbors time to prepare. Two days sound fine. The project is going to stay down indefinitely. He knows the repercussions and he is ready to justify his decision. Thank you."

"It's a go Pi. They are preparing a global shut down of all of the satellites' signals. They're going to be on high alert for any unforeseen problems. I hope and pray there aren't any though."

"So do I John. So do I."

"I guess you're wondering why I e-mailed you at this particular time for you to come and see me Misha. It's the uncertainty of the next two days that's got me to thinking about you, about me, and about us. It is exactly at a moment like this that I realize that I just want to be with someone who I really care about in this very special time of guesses and doubts. I don't know what the reversal of the project is going to have on the earth's population in two days. I just know I wanted to spend this time with you. I'm very much concerned . . ."

"Just relax and enjoy me Pi while you can."

"Hello Misha, I'm so glad that you could come to see me. My mother said you were coming today. I've been a little down lately."

"Oh no, what's wrong Pi?"

"The closer I get to my release date, the sadder I get. I know that really sounds strange, doesn't it? It should be the opposite way around but it's got so cumbersome on me in here until I felt like giving up. I thought the time that I was going to spend in here was going to fly by rather quickly but I seem to feel totally out of phase or something in here. It's very difficult to explain."

"Know this Pi; I'm waiting for you when you do get out. OK?"

"OK. At least now I have something to look forward to."

"I don't like it when you sound depressed like that Pi. What can I do?"

"Just let me touch you to see if you're really here."

"Mr. Dunavant, I don't understand it! You said Daniels probably had the artifact, didn't you? You also said he probably had something to do with Thornton disappearance but I just don't see it. Don't get me wrong; I know you are absolutely right about everything as you have been on all of our cases in the past, but for some reason; this time seems aberrant to a certain extent. Daniels surely does seem innocent doesn't he? The sheer fact that he is behind bars should have been an opening for us to get him to talk. I threatened him with some more jail time, with physical abuse and I came very close to threatening his life. He knew what I was saying and I didn't even see him blink. Could there be two scenarios here? One, where he actually believes he's telling the truth and the other scenario where he is a schizophrenic and actually is guilty and the version of him we see is his opposite self? I know it's straining at straws but what else could it be?"

Dunavant takes off his fedora and scratches his head.

"What? You've got to be kidding me! Even you have gone too far this time Mr. Dunavant. How can he be in two places at one time? This is our real life. This is no science fiction movie. Come on, we don't have much time with this case. We're standing on the verge of losing millions. You've never let me down before, except for that one time. This isn't the same situation, is it? That case was so bizarre. I thought about that case for so long and so hard until I can barely remember the basic details of it anymore. I remember his name and I remember that we were hired to find his whereabouts. You concluded that his whole ordeal was caused by stimulations received from intensified visual optics effects derived from some type of eye glasses. We followed your suggested leads until we came upon a recessed cave located underground which was a dead end. It was like he dropped off the face of the earth and there was no more Phillip Donaldson! Please Mr. Dunavant; don't let this case be like that one!"

"Pi, we have seventeen hours before the satellites shut down. Where have you been?"

"I was with Misha; I e-mailed her and told her that I needed to see her and that I needed to be with her for awhile. We don't really know what the results are going to be when the satellites shut down. You should go home and be with Peggy. How is she anyway?" "I haven't told her about any possible complications from side effects or anything like that, if that's what you mean. She's just happy with us."

"Good. Keep it that way. There's nothing else that you can do here. Go on home and be with Peggy Lee. Tell her I send my love. Get yourself a nice bottle of wine and just relax for awhile. Go on and get on out of here."

"Are you sure Pi? What if some of the international group call wanting to talk to you? You still can't talk on the phone Pi." "I told you don't worry about any of that. There's Stanley over there doing nothing. I got George outside. If they say they want to go home, then I'll let them go too. Some of the group will want to stay here just out of curiosity. Keep your cell phone charged up and keep a full tank of gas. If you need me for anything, just give me a high alert buzz on my laptop or text me on my cell. Just go home!"

"I'll hopefully see you tomorrow Pi."

"You mean *day after tomorrow.*"

"Yeah, right, *day after tomorrow.*"

"Group, listen up. I sent John home for two days. Anybody else, who needs to leave, can go. There is very little else that we can do here now but wait for the satellites to shut down. I have told all of you before that we don't exactly know what to expect after the satellites shut down because we didn't foresee having to shut them down at all. However, it's always safer to err on the side of caution so; since you all took the injections, if you want to remain here in the complex for it to be used as sort of a command center should the need arise to use the facility as such; you are more than welcome to remain here with me until we have determined that everything is in order."

"I'm staying," said Stanley.

"Me too," added George.

"We all are staying Pi, offered Sara."

"It's good to have a little company. I'm just going to go out for a little while. Stanley, you're in charge until I get back. If anything comes up, which I doubt it will; text me on the alert frequency, ok?"

"OK Pi. Where are you going?"

"Nowhere in particular really. I've just got to get some fresh air and take in a few sights. I should be back in a couple of hours. See y'all when I get back. Hold down the fort."

There is a saying that is very old and yet somehow, it still rings true today. God forgives but man don't.

Pilates headed directly to the hardware store and purchased ten five gallon gasoline cans with two twelve fluid ounce containers of lighter fluid. He purchased three cigarette lighters and one baseball bat and he placed all of the items into his van and headed to the nearest gasoline pump where he immediately began to fill all of the cans with fuel. He also took quite a large portion of the blue tinted paper towel from the dispenser located besides the pump with him as well. He then proceeded inside and paid the attending clerk, one hundred and eighty dollars with his credit card, and afterwards exited the store as if he were in no rush at all to leave. He methodically drove along the shaded streets under the high arching oaks, appearing to be merely sightseeing along the way. Every once in awhile, he would glance in his rear view mirror as one would normally do, to follow the traffic patterns that were emerging behind him. But of course, he was looking for something entirely different than traffic patterns. Pilates did not want to be followed at this time by anyone he knew or by the police.

He knew exactly where he was headed and he knew exactly what he was going to do once he arrived at his destination. First things first, he would start with the first floor and extend to the second and then finally finish at the third and top floor. He didn't want to murder anyone which was more than he could say about Archer's machine but if Archer showed up while he was fully engaged, well; he had to be prepared for that eventuality too. Thus, the veritable old baseball bat was readily at his disposal. He finally saw his intended destination ahead in the distance. He parked his van on a side street and waited for the brilliant sunshiny day to fade into the twilight duskiness of ebonic night. The activity of the past few days had caught up with Pilates while he waited for the night to arrive; and so consequently he fell asleep.

The seventeen hours countdown for the shutdown of the satellites had rolled around unceremoniously and Pilates was not awake to observe its passing. He only began to stir when he heard strange sounds emanating from outside of his van. Still partially asleep, he peeped through a reverie haze out of the van's window and saw figures harping about on the quiet streets of the neighborhood.

He jolted to attention at the uneasy feeling he began to experience from witnessing the uncomfortable sight. He immediately had the oddest sensation of being back in Sydney Green Minimum Security facility, where he had seen unspeakable horrors in the daytime; only now he was alone on Archer's street at night. Then a cold chill went up Pilates' spine as he slowly eyed his watch. The time had passed for the satellites to shut down. He had slept through it all! Pilates was curious about the outcome for the termination of his Project. He got out of his van and slowly walked down the sidewalks of the oak lined street. The moonlit silhouette figures that congregated around in mulling circles must surely have been the normal residents of this suburban community. They were in neither an alive nor dead state but an in between state; just as the inmates of the Sydney Green facility had been. Yet, these figures weren't standing completely still as the inmates had stood. These people were rapidly nodding their heads as if they were all agreeing with someone over and over again. *Not Zombies!* Pilates thought. He slowly tried to retreat back to his van without alerting them to his presence but they turned without provocation at Pilates' first surreptitious steps toward his van. They made no attempt to move towards Pilates in a menacing motion but he felt threatened by them anyway. Contrary to the way the inmates had looked, with their blank fixed stare; these people had a sinister gaze about them that projected a sheer malevolence. Pilates now noticed that the entire community had seemed to gather en masse on this particular street. All of them were nodding and bobbing and looking directly at him. A quiet resignation firmly came upon Pilates as he suddenly realized that he wasn't going to be able to escape this horde no matter how hard he tried to get away. He knew what he had to do, even if it meant losing his life in the process; it had to be done. He had to burn Archer's house down! Pilates knew it wasn't his project that had caused this travesty. It was Archer's machine that was responsible. He wished he and the doc could have found out exactly how Archer did it, but now he would never know.

Pilates eased his way back to his van very slowly. Then he started it, and maneuvered very delicately around the bystanders, who were now beginning to crowd the entire street so that it was virtually impossible for him or anything to exit the community. Pilates pulled his van into Archer's Driveway. He grabbed his gas cans and placed them on the driveway so that they were quickly accessible to him. He grabbed his bat and other supplies and started a rapid dousing of Archer's enormous home. Pilates proceeded to place cans all around the home. He tore off the tops of each of the cans and lit the blue paper towels and threw the lighter fluid container through an upstairs' window. Pilates stood back and watched the blaze ascend in spiraling torrents upwards into the night's sky. He wondered if Archer was home or not. Pilates screamed out in a loud voice: *I lit a fire under the machine and waited outside until it screamed!*

Pilates waited outside for a few moments before looking around to see that he was now completely *engulfed* by the zombie residents.

"Director Mulberry, we're about to let Daniels go. Do you want to say a few words to him before he leaves?"

"As a matter of fact I do Joe. Wait a minute while I wrap this up. Ok. I'm all done. Where is he?"

"He's outside the dorms sir."

"Oh good, I see him. Hey Pilates, I just wanted to say a few words to you before you are released. I know you had a tough few months with us but I hope we all had a learning experience from this situation. We've never had anyone with your caliber in here before. You put us on the map as far as bragging rights for who has housed the most famous inmate. Have you contacted your people for your ride home?"

"I haven't. For some strange reason, no one has contacted me about my release. I'm not too worried though because I can always walk to town."

"Yeah, but that's about three hours of walking Pilates. I can call someone to see what the problem is; if that's alright with you?" "I guess so Director Mulberry."

"That's very peculiar. All of the lines are down. I'm sorry Pilates but all of the lines are down."

"That's ok. I really can walk."

"Alright, if you insist. Be careful out there and remember; I don't want to ever see you back in here again."

"You won't."

"Joe, open the gates."

"Yes sir. Hey, I wonder what's going on in town. It looks like something caught on fire. Man, look at that blaze Director."

"I believe you're right Joe. It looks like someone dropped a bomb or something, doesn't it? Wait a minute Pilates. Do you think you ought to go into town now with all of that going on? It sure does seem strange.

We should have heard some reports or something about this. Joe, check the television. Maybe they have the story on what's going on."

"Director, I really need to go. I'll be alright. If it's ok with you, I'll be on my way.

"Ok. Ok. Guard, let the inmate out."

Pilates left Sidney Green Minimum security lockup with a curious and pensive mind. Freedom at last. He immediately breathed in the burnt aroma of burning rags and noticed the darkened sky, brimming with odors that hinted at a mixture of sulfur and chlorine. What could this be, he pondered? He began a slow steady trot towards town, feeling a somewhat urgent desire to understand it all at once. Now he could sense sooty black embers falling all around him. His trotting soon developed into a galloping sprint as he nervously perceived the seriousness of the moment. Suddenly, he heard voices upon voices, gregariously speaking all around him with diffused screaming in the tumult of his darkening surroundings. The wind arose stiffly and bore up a spinning wall of dust and debris, churning eddies after eddies in ever ascending walls of parched air upwards into the agitated sky. Pilates felt his heart racing as if it were going to burst inside his chest while the pang from his throbbing head ached like something that he had never felt before. The air soon became so dense and so dusty that Pilates had to stop to try to catch his breath. Because of the soot and dust and smoke, he could not get his bearings as to which way to go; he could not see anything at all. *One world, one mind and one voice!* Drawing strength and resolve from his mantra, Pilates took a deep breath and began anew his galloping dash across the plains of Sumer and Shinar.